A CASUALTY OF WILDFLOWERS

A SEA OF ECHOES NOVELLA

A SEA OF ECHOES
BOOK 1.5

MISTY D. WATERS

EDITED BY
KERRI DOYLE ~ DARK BEAR MEDIA

A Sea of Echoes is a fictional world that borrows naming conventions, styles, and religions from various cultures, ancient and recent-past, from all over the world. None of them are meant to be an accurate representation of any point in history.

You can find a list of **trigger warnings** here:

Pronunciation guide and other details here:

DEDICATION

This is for the TikTok Book Club—you know who you are. You lifted me from my lowest low and motivated me to get myself up, shake the dust off, and get to writing. I will forever be grateful to all of you.

PROLOGUE

The Royal Guard chased one of their own through the East Harbor Market. The five men, outfitted in the leather, blue, and silver of their station, barreled over innocents without regard. Moonlight reflected off the sweat that coated their faces and necks.

Oskar Dahlin, Master Blade of the Assassin's Guild, hung his head from where he perched inside a temple tower. His palace contacts were already down to scant numbers, and the man they chased, Elias, had been one of his best.

It can't wait, Elias's note had said. The quick scrawl lacking in both details and careful planning revealed how dire this information was. That its importance couldn't be shared in something as permanent as script. Elias wasn't only risking his life but those of his wife and daughters, who would be gathered and enslaved by morning as punishment. A warning to anyone else who considered defying the king.

Oskar watched long enough to realize that Elias led his followers with intention. Even in his desperation to escape, Elias acted rationally. Drawing them ever closer to where Oskar was meant to be waiting, the only aid Elias would find.

Except, instinct had led Oskar to the Temple of the Gods tonight to watch Elias's back. Oskar had worried the guard might be followed, but not *chased*.

Oskar backtracked through the temple—a lethal shadow—and burst from a side door into the streets. Dust and gravel kicked up under his boots. He took more care to avoid a collision, taking to the roofs where he could, needing every advantage. Elias's life—and the information he carried—depended on his timely arrival.

Elias was already engaged in battle by the time Oskar reached him. The guards' swords a furious stroke, Elias at their center. Tiring. Slowing.

Oskar entered the fight, easily breaking a neck on the way to meeting another with a pair of Kopis knives, just as a spear sank into Elias's gut. Elias fell into a table of vases and bowls, the entire lot going down with a clamber of shattering clay.

Failure twisted through Oskar like a cyclone, yet he continued his battle against the remaining guardsmen. He doubted the king knew who Elias was meeting, and Oskar needed it to stay that way.

Oskar let his body fall into its natural rhythm for the next few minutes. He spun into the shift of air and toward the slice of steel, letting his senses protect him. He took the jarring hits with his blades, feeding off the vibrations up his arms. The dead fell around him in the wake of his arcing knives, but he refused to let those thoughts distract him.

Then...silence. The world stilled, and he was left with only his heaving breaths and a dull ache in his palms.

He knelt at Elias's side. The young man—relatively young only to Oskar's five and fifty years—made quick gasping sounds, his hands failing to staunch the flow of blood.

Oskar added his hands to the man's wound. "What's happened?"

Elias gasped for air. "My wife, Marietta— The girls—"

"I'll see to their safety. I swear it." Oskar had, at most, an hour to relocate the family. Based on the blood loss, Elias's color, and his shallow breath, he wouldn't last a full minute. "Don't let your secret die with you, friend. Tell me what was so urgent."

Elias coughed, and blood sprayed across his lips and chin. He gripped the side of Oskar's neck, eyes widening. "Northeast tower." He swallowed, his throat bobbing low. "The true king lives, Oskar. Mihail li—"

The man choked and convulsed, then went utterly still. Eyes open but unseeing.

Oskar shook the dead man, his mind spiraling and the ground tilting. His heart pounded with new life. "Elias! What do you mean?"

Elias was gone.

"Master?" Stefanos Andretis stood like a wraith in the nearby shadow, outfitted in solid black with a hood over his head. His identical twin, Panos, watched their backs. The brothers must have witnessed Oskar's race through the marketplace and come running.

Oskar laid Elias down and closed the man's dead eyes. *The true king lives.* Gods, was it possible?

Now wasn't the time to get lost in the prospect. He had a death promise to keep.

He scrubbed his face with an aching, bruised hand, then stood and faced the twins. "Gather some men. This man's family is in danger."

He quickly shared the details with the young assassins, who followed his command. Marietta and her daughters would be squirreled safely away long before Orestis's men breached their doorstep.

Usually, acting against Orestis lifted Oskar's spirits—anything to trip up the king and his heinous acts against his people—but his mind clung to Elias's final words.

The true king lives.

The true king lives.

Mihail is alive.

Impossible.

In the distance, looming high over Praevia's market, the palace glowed with candlelight. The tower jutting out of the northeast corner was but a cold, black monolith. The perfect place to imprison someone away from prying eyes. Away from the usual host of prisoners in the palace bowels and its rotation of guards.

Orestis kept a lot of secrets, but this? Was he capable of faking his own twin's death? Keeping him alive all these years? Why? For what reason—?

The truth struck him low in the gut.

The prophecy.

The true heir.

This was it, wasn't it?

The time had finally come.

E manouella Vidalatos despised Court. She'd never found a foothold in the bland politics—that weren't politics at all—of the Perean noblewomen, which were superfluous at best. Her mother's influence held nothing to her father's, who'd placed her on his lap during council meetings. Never thinking twice about the idea that she'd hold an interest in Soterran politics the way only men seemed to.

Her husband, Orestis, would never include her in matters of state and had made that known in the early days of their marriage. She'd been two and ten at the time, a foolish, hopeful child believing her new husband and king—crowned only the year prior—to be a better man than her brother, Titos.

Emanouella drifted through the room with her handmaid in tow. Speaking when spoken to. Laughing and smiling when expected. Granting kindness and blessings wherever necessary. Mostly, though, she listened.

Something had the Council gathered in a tight formation, speaking in whispers. It didn't bode well that they excluded Orestis from whatever had them in this tense thrall. Had Orestis trusted her, given her more slack on her leash, she might have alerted him. But his ability to lead and garner trust was no longer her concern. He could hang for all she cared.

A member of her Queen's Guard approached with an envelope. "This has just arrived for Her Majesty."

"Thank you."

Her heart thrummed wildly, and her breath turned ragged. She held the parchment to her chest and glanced around as if anyone would easily guess its contents.

Hot tears pricked her eyes. He hadn't given up. He was still there. Still her ally. Her friend. Her—

"Are you all right, my lady?" Tasia asked. She was a young woman with black skin, hair shorn to the scalp, and had been with Emanouella only a few short months. Plucked from the streets without a home, family, or friends.

"I'm fine, thank you."

"Is that"—she nodded pointedly at the folded parchment—"another one?"

Yes, it was. She didn't have to open it to know what lay inside. Even so, she couldn't help but break the seal and spread the folds. A single blue flower petal slid out and floated to the ground. Not a single word marred the pearl-colored paper.

Tasia picked up the stray petal. "Could this be an admirer?"

"It's a harmless gesture." Emanouella folded the edges back around the flower. "I think I will retire to the garden for a while."

"I will get your—"

"No need." Emanouella tamped down the swell of happiness threatening to overload her senses. It wouldn't do to draw anyone's attention. "Have you seen Selene?"

"No, ma'am. Should I pass on a message?"

"No, I'll find her. Take the afternoon for yourself, thank you."

Tasia's tawny eyes sparked. She'd recently started speaking with a young fisherman in secret. Emanouella suspected they were more than fond of each other and found no need to interfere in their happiness. Besides, Emanouella benefited from her excursions as well.

Tasia curtsied and left the room, skirting the outer walls until she disappeared through the exit.

Emanouella also made to leave when a sharp slap startled half the room.

Inside an alcove, just past a wide marble column, Alexandra raised her hand to strike her handmaid a second time—

Emanouella started toward her vicious, cruel daughter, but a large, calloused hand snapped around her wrist.

She looked into the cold, gray eyes of Apollon Rodelis. "Unhand me."

"Her Majesty the Queen wouldn't want to interfere with matters that are none of her concern." The temple priest smiled, and his attention lowered to the valuable item in her hand. He snatched her precious envelope and held it out of her automatic reach.

Emanouella understood what it must feel like for Alexandra to give over to every whim. She longed for the relief of the sting her palm would feel across his cheek. Or the warmth of his blood. "You have no right—"

"Let's not draw attention," Apollon warned conspiratorially, absently opening the paper. The lone petal fell for the second time. The High Priest bent to retrieve it, his thick, wiry brows drawn together. "What have we here?"

<hr>

Hours later, the setting sun deepening the colors in the field of wildflowers, Emanouella lowered her cloak's hood. A balmy breeze off the nearby bluff whipped through her hair and plastered the silks of her apricot-colored chiton against her legs.

She navigated the path through the field, past the ivory-barked forest's tree line where the air cooled within, and true darkness had fallen beneath the lush canopy. But she knew the way by heart, and there was nothing to fear.

The tiny cottage appeared around the bend, and she quickened her steps with her heart and head light. She crossed the threshold and entered the familiar space, hiding the quiver of her hands behind her back.

Oskar rose from the bench at the small table across the room. "Hi."

Emanouella settled her back against the closed door. "Hi."

PART ONE

A ROSE AMONG THORNS

I

Twenty-two Years Ago

It was the sort of crisp, mild morning one might expect between winter and spring. Warmth would be in full bloom by midday, then cold again by nightfall. Not unlike the lands where Oskar had spent the last eight years, only Perean had a fraction of the rain.

Oskar stepped off the skiff and into Hristos Martas's waiting arms. The years might have changed Hristos physically, but the man still carried a way about him that put Oskar at ease. Hristos was a tall and imposing figure—Oskar had seen the best of the King's Guard balk in his presence—but a sharp kindness filled the man's eyes. His arms were strong, and his hands deadly when called upon, but his touch could also be gentle and guiding.

Hristos was an enigma to most, but not Oskar. He was the father Oskar never knew and had taught him to walk through the darkest paths without corruption. To be a man who was gentle and understanding. Only true goodness balanced the unpleasantness of their profession. Otherwise, they were lost.

The thrill of seeing his mentor again might have split Oskar's chest in two. "Your hair has gone all white, old man," he said through small bursts of laughter. "Have I been gone that long?"

Hristos, only somewhat taller, pulled away just enough to look Oskar warmly in the eye. "Eight years hasn't left you untouched, either. You left here a boy and have returned a man."

Oskar didn't feel so unchanged on the inside, though he knew what time had unleashed on his exterior. Gray strands of hair colored his temples. Years of relentless training had hewn quite a bit more muscle. And maybe, just maybe, his calmer mind showed in his expression and the set of his shoulders. His time away had been meant to heal old wounds under the guise of further discipline, and it had. At the very least, he'd learned to separate his actions from his emotions.

Hristos cupped Oskar's head. "Welcome home."

Home, at the moment, was no more than a gritty, damp beach and a small cove. A mile-high cliff walled them off from the capital city itself. Last he was in Praevia, he'd have gladly burned everything to the ground and happily gone with it.

Yes, he'd come a long way since then.

"Come," Hristos said, slinging Oskar's one sack of belongings over a shoulder. "You're home in time for the festival and games."

The telltale signs of celebration had been viewed from the ship. Even if he hadn't already seen the bright-colored flags, he'd have guessed by the number of visitors arriving in the harbor. People came from all over for the games, both to watch and risk their lives for the honor of calling themselves the victor.

"Which god are we honoring for the next week?" he asked.

"The ocean god, Soris." Hristos trudged across the sand toward a nearly invisible path in the seagrass. "The palace has many royal visitors this week."

There would be an increase in City Guard, then. The harbor market would be drowning in vendors from all over the kingdom, which meant more "accidents" at the hands of emboldened guardsmen.

"Just let me know where I'm needed," Oskar said.

"You've been traveling for two months. Take the day to rest. Take the entire week if needed," Hristos added with a shrug. "You're no good to your brothers without a temperate mind."

"Wasn't that the point of shipping me off to Linesh? To master myself in body and mind and soul? I'm always ready. It matters not that I've been traveling."

Hristos gave him a thorough scan, then nodded. "I stand corrected. Maybe it is I who needs some time to adjust and reconcile your changes." After another moment, he said, "I could use another man in the market later today. Half of the continent will be celebrating the opening festivities. Let's get you settled first, though. Will you be staying with your brothers?"

Oskar had wondered what his answer to that question would be for the last two months. As young, new acolytes, the men stayed together. Trained, ate, and slept as one. They were a family.

However, the time always came when a man grew up and longed for independence. Being a Blade didn't require a vow of celibacy, nor did he shun the idea of taking a wife. Building a family was encouraged, though few had.

For now, Oskar had no desire for more than what his Guild family offered, but he did long for his own space. "Nikos and Natalia had a cottage. Do you know if it still stands?"

Oskar's best friend had been dead for… Had it truly been seven and ten years already? It felt like yesterday.

In any case, Oskar had spent many a night thinking of that little home Nikos had built for his wife. Hidden inside the woods with a trail leading to a bluff of wildflowers that overlooked Praevia. One didn't have to travel long to reach their cottage, but once there, the entire world felt an eternity away.

Hristos's brow furrowed, and his words came with the slightest hesitation. "I assume it's still there. Why do you ask?"

"I imagine it will need some maintenance, but I like to think Nikos wouldn't mind if I lived there."

"He would not," Hristos confirmed, a sad smile spread his lips. "He loved you more than most."

And Oskar, him. Nikos had been more than his best friend. He'd been a true brother. Not by blood, of course, but by soul. Three years had separated them in age, but somehow, that had never mattered. Nikos had guided Oskar as a brother would, whether in the ways of the Guild or the ways around a woman's body.

Nikos had been the one to hand Oskar his first ale. Had taught him to fish. Once, as foolish young boys, they'd traveled to the nearest family of seers and ran screaming before the old woman with one eye and gnarled fingers got a hand on them. Laughing about their shared cowardice the entire way home.

Oskar had been there the day Nikos fell for a pretty silk merchant with his strange, mismatched eyes.

And it was Oskar who'd spent much of his elder youth searching for answers to their disappearance. He never found them. It was widely assumed that Nikos and Natalia had left, but Oskar knew in his heart that something happened. Nikos wouldn't have left him without a word.

Then everyone was distracted by the war against Otuvia, followed later by the death of King Minos. Then the coronation of Prince Orestis, and his child bride, Emanouella, who'd been only two and twelve. Why would anyone care about a missing Blade of the Assassin's Guild?

Hristos approached with eyes that burrowed straight into Oskar's soul, searching and questioning. "Do I need to worry about this choice of yours?"

Nikos had been the reason Oskar was sent away for reflection. Oskar hoped Hristos believed him as he said, "No. I have accepted he's gone." It was a truth that had taken years for him to accept. "If the gods wish me to know how or why, they will place those truths at my feet when I am ready to hear them and not a moment before."

Lines and grooves disappeared from Hristos's expression. "Your time away has made you wise, then, and I have no reason for concern. Shall I take the journey with you? We can gauge what work needs to be done together."

Oskar gave a single nod. "I would appreciate any help you would offer. Thank you, Hristos. Truly."

Hristos set an arm across Oskar's shoulders and urged them back into a walk. "We can discuss your future with our order on the way."

Oskar knew the cottage would be in a rough state based solely on the overgrown path. Grass rose as high as his knees, and if there were still flowers on the bluff, it was too early in the year for their wild bloom, but he'd know for sure in a matter of days.

He'd ended up alone for the journey—Hristos had been drawn back to the market by a young pair of acolytes. It had been for the best. Returning to Nikos and Natalia's home was sure to bring back any number of emotions, and he didn't want Hristos to think he wasn't okay.

Oskar had truly changed and grown during his time away. The desperate desire to spend his days on a fruitless path was long gone. He would move forward and honor the Guild and be of service to his people as he'd been brought up to be.

Just as he began the route into the forest toward the cottage, a warm breeze wrapped around him, drenched in the scent of the sea and sweet temple smoke. Before he knew it, he was on the cliff's edge. Far below, Praevia was vibrant with the king's colors: blue and silver. The land was separated by patches of color; the brown and green of farmed land, and the gray and grit of the city.

The hum of human excitement carried on the wind, almost beckoning him toward the varieties of wine and ale, the prepared delicacies, and any number of women available, for the right price. It'd been a while since he lay with anyone; tonight was as good a time as any to break that streak.

Tension leaked from his shoulders, and all weight vanished. This must be what it felt like to float above the world. This view, these sounds, the chaos awaiting him...this was his life. These were his people. And his Guild brothers were down there, watching it all from the comforting shadows.

Oskar rubbed his inner wrist and the familiar ridged brand given to all Blades of the Guild: a bird in flight crossed by a longsword. He and Nikos had gotten theirs in the same place.

"I'm home, brother," he said into the wind. To Nikos. "Maybe I'm not the same man I was when I left. But I'll be honest, I'm no less alone without you by my side." What he couldn't say aloud was that he feared that would never change.

"I hope you don't mind me living in your little shack." He chuckled over the running joke of his youth. He'd needled Nikos for months. "I did help you build it, after all. And if I have to rebuild it from scratch because you couldn't be bothered to look after it, I'm going to be slightly irate with you."

Oskar brushed the tall grass with his palm, and a velvety knob broke the bend of pliant strips. A single blue budding flower stretched its petals against its outer shell, seeking a way out.

This truly was a new beginning.

This was hope.

Oskar smiled and started for home.

***

"To another son," Orestis toasted boastfully from the head of the table, a goblet raised toward Emanouella.

Emanouella smiled. At least she gave it her best attempt. She wasn't fooling anyone. One look at her handmaid, Chrysanthi, told her that. The young woman stood with all the other attendants across the dining room, her gaze darting to the king and back.

If any of their guests saw beyond her mask, they couldn't guess the extent of the truth, surely.

Emanouella had lost another child.

Orestis would be furious, and she couldn't stomach his rage so soon. She wished to mourn her loss first. Besides, this personal tragedy wasn't the business of the visiting royals.

Her brother Titos, the king of Soterra, would especially have something condescending to add. Words like blades through her skin about her failure as a wife and queen. What would their poor, dead father have to say? He'd then twist the knife with how it was a good thing their father hadn't lived long enough to witness his perfect daughter's deficient womb. It would kill him all over again.

Titos narrowed his eyes from his seat across the table as if sensing the direction of her thoughts. He had the place of honor on Orestis's left side.

"It appears to be a theme," the king of Crudea said. He was an obnoxiously loud man whose wife laughed at nearly everything he said. They formed a strange pair who had an opinion on literally everything, from the flower choices in Emanouella's prized garden to Orestis's commissioned marble likeness for the games. The twenty-foot statue stood in the harbor, greeting travelers from all over the world.

"It's almost as if," his wife added with good humor, "you men planned to impregnate us on purpose for this very visit."

Indeed, Titos's wife Violeta was heaviest with their fourth child. The empress of Tineian and the matriarch of Yiria were also showing.

While the kings and leaders of seven visiting kingdoms turned this into a lively discussion about each man's prowess, their eighth royal guest, the matriarch of Yiria, leaned over to speak to Emanouella privately.

"I hope you won't include us in this offense," Shadi said with a gesture that included her wife Doli and their male consort Tse. The three of them gave a respectful nod. "To bear a child is a blessing from the gods themselves and not the choice of a human man." She scowled. "Even if they call themselves king."

Emanoulla choked back a laugh. This was her first time meeting someone from Yiria. When she learned these three had been assigned seats beside her at the table, she wondered if someone had intentionally placed them there to make her uncomfortable. After all, the Yirians were culturally very different from everyone else at the table.

It was said that the solid black circle between their brows was a mark of their clan. The matriarch, Shadi, had an additional tattoo: a stylized wolf shaped as if by the wind on her left cheek, just below her eye.

As for their manner of dress, handcrafted hides and furs in browns, grays, and ochres made up their entire wardrobes. No dyed silks or cotton. Red maclinite gems and turquoise stones completed their ensembles in necklaces, bracelets, and anklets.

According to their limited knowledge of the world, Yiria was the only queendom in existence, and the females outnumbered the males two to one. It was on Emanouella to ensure they felt welcome and likely to keep them out of everyone else's way.

To Emanouella's surprise, this interaction instantly made her like and trust the matriarch. "Don't tell my husband," Emanouella replied quietly, "but I agree. Although, I fear the gods have plans that don't align with his, and that fault will fall on me regardless of the outcome."

Shadi's attention fell on Emanouella's stomach. Emanouella nodded at her raised, questioning brow.

The young matriarch squeezed Emanouella's hand beneath the table. "May the winds guide their sweet soul safely home."

Heat pricked behind her eyes. "Thank you."

"We should speak later. Maybe a tour of your gardens? Doli mentioned how pleasant they are."

The woman beside her smiled. She had the same dark brown hair and eyes as her wife and their consort. "I hope you don't mind. Tse and I walked through them earlier. We don't have anything like this back home."

"Because you dwell inside a mountain," Titos said, his voice carrying through the room like a barge. When had he started eavesdropping on their conversation? "Like heathens."

Chortles of laughter followed the insult.

Emanouella stiffened. The Yirians weren't a weak people; the females were renowned warriors. If Shadi—or Doli or Tse, for that matter—responded physically, Emanouella sat too close for comfort.

Shadi cut calmly into her meat and raised the fork to her mouth. "As you say, Your Majesty."

Her wife and consort continued eating from their plates as well, wholly unbothered.

Emanouella met her brother's heated gaze and released her first genuine smile of the evening.

⸻

The market was alive all around Emanouella, with the festival in full swing. No one paid mind to the cloaked woman weaving through the crowds. She preferred it this way and always had.

As one of them, she saw life as it was. It wasn't organized or subdued. No one put on airs, and they danced wherever they pleased. They ate standing up, drank reclined against walls, and laughed until they fell. Bawdy tunes carried into the street from full taverns.

She envied them the freedom of it all. Even—maybe even *especially*—the couples having sex inside alleyways. They clearly enjoyed it, and after years of marriage, she had no idea why. She was clearly missing something.

One truth stood out above all as she journeyed through the

streets: here, she was free to be whoever she wanted. In the palace, she was a trussed up womb for a king's pleasure. Early in their marriage, she honestly believed she loved her husband. That if she were bright enough, elegant enough, bold enough, he would love her in return. As if she were a jewel only he could polish.

She knew better now that she was older. Orestis was incapable of such a thing, which was no fault of hers.

By the time she reached her destination, night had nearly fallen. The Temple of the Gods was second only to the palace itself in grandeur. White columns held up the gold-peaked roof, and smoke climbed toward the gods from dozens of open prayer chambers.

Emanouella wished to share her prayers with the gods as well. It didn't matter who heard them as long as she could empty herself of this consuming darkness.

Inside the temple, young, robed acolytes circled the perimeter with their hands in constant prayer. They kept the candles lit for the High Priest, Apollon Rodelis, who was, thankfully, back at the palace. He was almost always with Orestis. She rarely recalled a time when he wasn't.

Priests also milled about the temple, some speaking to the devout who searched for guidance.

Emanouella only wished for the peace to mourn in sight of the gods. There were plenty of them to choose from in the surrounding alcoves, but she sat on a marble bench inside the shadows at the back and lowered her cloak hood.

She wore no indications of wealth, and her hair was long and loose to her waist. Her gray chiton had once belonged to a handmaid and was made from cheap material rather than the silks she was accustomed to. As a child, she'd watched her mother perform this "magic trick" to become a commoner on multiple occasions. Her mother would whisper conspiratorially that it was their little secret.

Emanouella never understood why or where her mother disappeared during those times, but she liked to think it was for similar reasons. To be someone unimportant for a while. To simply be a woman who dreamed. Not a queen or a wife or a mother; not that she regretted her son Angelos. In the five years he'd been alive, he was the one person in the world who loved her without condition.

The one person.

An ache filled her chest, and the fractures she'd sensed splintering all day suddenly had nowhere left to go. Hot tears burst from her eyes. And because she was safely away from all those who would judge, she let the grief spill and spill and spill.

Later, when her eyes had dried and she could stomach the idea of returning home, she stood and reached for her hood—

A spot of blue on the white marble caught her eye. A flower, recently budded. It hadn't been there when she sat down.

Emanouella lifted the stem and brought the flower to her nose. Its fragrance was no more than a ghost of its potential, but was just the reminder she needed. There were endings, but there were also beginnings.

Maybe, just maybe, the spring ahead could be hers.

2

Oskar slunk unseen through the shadows of the colosseum to the distant sounds of an excitable crowd preparing for the games' opening event. Nothing had changed since he last came through. The guards were still posted in the same areas and, unsurprisingly, few knew about the secret passageways behind the marble statues on the outer tier rings. Perean was full of secrets like this, all forgotten by time but recorded and preserved by centuries of Guild Masters.

Eventually, Oskar came to the interior rings of the amphitheater and blinked into the sharp sunlight. Several concrete tiers made up the oval shape, each designated to certain classes. He walked down the slope of stairs to the first level, the one closest to the dirt-coated ground meant for the upper classes—courtiers, members of the king's council, and those similar in class from visiting countries.

They were spread out across the two lower tiers, outfitted in their finest silks, perfumed and layered in their best jewelry pieces. They were protected by three times as many guards as the upper tiers, where the poorest were crammed together.

Oskar was dressed similarly, so no one questioned him when he settled amongst them. From his vantage point, he had a direct view of the royal podium built into the second tier—an open, shaded floor with an unobstructed view of the entire stadium. Some of the royal visitors had arrived early and taken their seats at the back, where they huddled in conversation.

With plenty of time left to spare, the men bet on the first game's outcome. A foolish waste of money. Slaves of little value would be armed and thrown into this battle at random because it was sure to be the bloodiest event of the week. The victor would be the last man standing, but they'd have to survive while also avoiding some manner of creature that had yet to be named.

The royal podium began filling as the event start drew near. Many men wore togas or chlamys over tunics, and the women wore either a chiton or stola. All except for three: the Yirian triad. They appeared as warriors outfitted in leather, fur, and weaponry. If they noticed the other royals scoffing at them, they paid it no heed.

At last, King Vidalatos entered with his queen on his arm.

Oskar took one look at her and had to do a double-take. A bark of laughter leapt from his chest, and he earned a narrowed look from his neighbor.

He reclined forward on his knees and tried rubbing his grin away. Who else knew their queen was a sly creature of the night? Had he not spent eight years away, he might have recognized her, but she'd been a child of two and ten last he saw her. Merely a girl sent to Perean to wed a man thirteen years her senior.

Emanouella Vidalatos was a woman now and, far and away, the most beautiful of the royals. Truly ethereal. Her chiton was of the purest white trimmed in gold, and her crown tall and ornate. Matching bracelets climbed her slim wrist, and earrings dangled to her bare shoulders.

What god had guided him to her last night? He'd thought her a slave—a beautiful one, at that—and he'd felt called to keep an eye on her up to the very moment she slunk back into the palace through a servants' entrance.

Oskar thought all night about how he'd plucked one of those budding blue flowers on the way back to the city yesterday. He'd walked by, snapped it mid-stem, and tucked it inside his cloak only to give it to the young, beautiful stranger in the temple.

Her anguish had acted like a mirror, reminding him of all the times he'd sat alone in his. With no one to sit with him or say the right words. No one to reflect with. And he couldn't do that with her, either—not without giving himself away. But he could give her a gift. The thing that had filled him with hope.

Now, here he was, full of questions. Starting with why the queen felt it necessary to hide a visit to the temple. Ending with, what happened to hurt her *that much*? Did she have no one in her life to talk to? At *all*?

From his vantage point, the answer was plain. Emanouella was surrounded by royals, including her brother and husband, yet no one looked her way. Only the Yirian triad, but they only offered her respectful nods from their distant seats near the back.

Oskar leaned toward the Perean lord beside him. "Is the queen a cruel woman?" With so many foreign visitors, no one would question why he asked.

The lord stiffened and barely turned toward him to offer a response. "The queen? Not that I'm aware of. Why do you ask?"

"They're all avoiding her." He gave a pointed nod to the open platform. "Curious, don't you think?"

The man shrugged, then turned back to his previous conversation. Not even this stranger could find one second of consideration for his queen.

Emanouella lowered into one of the two front seats and folded her hands atop her lap, a smile painted on her face. Oskar couldn't find any truth in her expression, and that, too, made him sad. She was no better than a painting that was ordered by a man, for a man.

The queen's gaze shifted through the lower tiers, then stopped abruptly on Oskar himself.

He should look away. Be the invisible man he was meant to be.

Instead, he smiled at her.

And Emanouella smiled back.

――――――

Emanouella didn't recognize the lord smiling at her, but that was true of almost everyone attending today.

Whoever he was, she credited him for the warm spring bubbling through her. She'd lived among handsome men her entire life—her husband included—and this man was no exception. Dark hair with hints of gray. Square, clean-shaven jaw. He was Orestis's age if she had to guess.

However, she'd never quite known anyone to live in their skin so...boisterously. He sat alone, occupying much space in his solitude rather than hiding within it. She always felt isolated, especially when surrounded by a crowd, and to have people see her that way made her wish to become invisible.

Orestis fell into the seat beside her like a giant gust of air. He beamed a smile into the crowd—no one could resist that smile. Not even her, once upon a time. "You could learn something from all the other wives," he muttered under his breath. "Instead of acting as if they're all beneath you, maybe you could try holding a conversation."

Another reason she wished to disappear. No one understood her. No one even tried. The women found her interests in local politics and the state of their people odd. Why was this any of her concern? Apparently, she should stick to her gardens and poetry and painting. It had always been this way, and she stopped trying long ago.

Once her ire was soundly contained, she said, "I will try to do better."

"You can try tonight while the royals meet to discuss a few matters."

"I didn't realize you all had so much to discuss."

Orestis swung his cloudy blue gaze her way. "Why would you?"

"You're right, of course. Forgive me."

An eruption of applause and cheers stole his attention. Below, twenty men strode through one of several gated doorways. They'd been outfitted in soldier garb and given one weapon apiece. Despite their lack of freedom to perform during this event, they played up to the people with smiles and weapons thrust toward the azure sky.

Orestis stood for his part, on the edge of it all, his hand lifted to quiet the crowd. "Good luck to you all!" he shouted, then signaled to the beastmaster. "May Soris bless the victor with a long life. For the rest of you, may Saenar guide and keep you in the Valley."

Several of the beastmaster's men came together at a wheel and turned the crank. The amphitheater floor shook, and the layer of dirt and sediment vibrated. The twenty participants who'd been standing toward the center, ran from the opening that parted in a long slit.

A deep pool appeared, reflecting the blue sky and billowing clouds.

Tentacles slid through the gap, and a collective gasp shot through the tiered levels.

"*What is that?*" one of the queens asked, horrified.

Orestis smiled. "A serpulagus—commonly referred to as an Imperial Squid. No need to worry. It's only a baby."

The "baby" that climbed out of the water was the length of two grown men from the top of its pointed head to the tips of its eight tentacles. The serrated hooks along its head gave the impression of a crown and were fully developed. Not only was it a swift-moving creature on land, but it could survive outside the water for up to two minutes.

The Perean people stood and cheered as the participants readied their weapons. Their fear was palpable. It would take all of them to kill the beast, let alone each other. If they were smart, they'd work together.

The serpulagus acted immediately, swinging at the nearest man armed with a poleaxe. A tentacle gripped him around the legs and lifted him high in the air before slamming him back down. The slave went limp. Surely, he was already dead when the squid stuffed him whole into the mouth that was hidden beneath its body.

Emanouella sat forward in her seat and gripped the arms. Not to get a closer look but because she was locked between fleeing and keeping appearances.

Bringing this creature into the games felt especially cruel. Orestis had been giddy for weeks while keeping the beast a secret. His beast-master must have had a dozen ships scouring the open sea to find this creature. How many had already died to have it contained in the underground pool?

The squid scrambled after fresh victims, eating two more before reentering the deep seawater pool. A fourth man was knocked in with the serpulagus and bobbed up seconds later near the middle. He discarded his weapon and arced his arms in great, heaving strokes toward the edge.

The whirlpool began in slow motion, and the squid was a blur of outspread tentacles on the bottom.

Eyes bulging, the swimmer hurried and was mere feet from the edge when the water cyclone yanked him under.

Blood clouded the pool, and the crowd gasped.

The serpulagus rose with the body hooked to its crown, limbs splayed in awkward angles. A tentacle pulled him off by one of his feet and brought him below the surface to its mouth.

Emanouella couldn't watch anymore, and her mouth filled with a sour taste she had difficulty swallowing.

The crowd cheered, screamed, and stomped, and she almost took the man's shout from behind as one of them. "For my king, Quintus Milonius Gregorius!"

Cold prickled down the back of her neck, and she spun toward the man bearing an unsheathed longsword. He was outfitted in the garb of a Perean soldier. One of their protectors.

The man drove the sword through her nephew Lambros, the crown prince of Soterra.

A curdling scream ripped from Queen Violeta. She was the first to reach for her falling son, a boy of three and ten, while others ducked or ran.

"Assassin!" someone yelled.

Emanouella leapt to her feet as two more of their Guard revealed themselves as traitors, turning their swords on the remaining royals.

The Yirian triad hurried the unarmed wives and children behind them, forming a blockade with their own bodies. Tse double-fisted a spear while Shadi and Doli pulled bone-handled blades from their back sheaths.

Orestis arced his sword between Emanouella and an assassin whose full attention held her in his cold grasp. Their steel clashed and slid. They glared through crossed pommels and pushed apart.

Orestis backed into Emanouella, and she lost her footing.

She hit the ground, and pain shot through her shoulder and wrist. All around her were men's sandaled or booted feet, shuffling forward and back. One pair heading right for her.

She rolled—

The floor disappeared, and Emanouella felt nothing but open air.

The Perean Royal Guard had been infiltrated by assassins. That much was immediately clear to Oskar.

The name they rallied and killed for was one Oskar hadn't heard in well over a decade. Quintus Gregorius had once been the king of Otuvia, a kingdom conquered by Perean and Soterran forces following the assassination of their two crown princes.

After all this time, Quintus had a score to settle, and it was lucky Orestis hadn't brought his five-year-old son to the event. Prince Angelos would undoubtedly be dead alongside the Soterran prince if he had.

The amphitheater was in chaos, and not everyone had realized that the royals were under attack. They were so fixated on the serpulagus that it took Queen Emanouella falling directly into the beast's pit for them to take notice.

Oskar quickly assessed the situation. Emanouella wouldn't last a single minute alone down there. But his mandate drummed within him like a second heartbeat. The Guild didn't interfere in the lives of the royals. Their safety never came before the Perean people and never *ever* before their own lives.

He couldn't ignore the tug, the push of an invisible hand toward her. The woman was a mirror to the man he might've been had his life gone differently. She was alone when she shouldn't have to be. No one cared to offer her a passing glance when she was breathing their same air, what would they do now that she was in grave danger?

One of the contenders raced toward the queen, and Oskar suddenly found it hard to breathe. He leaned forward as if he could lend strength and speed to the man. All sounds split between moments of before and after, vanishing altogether in that single heartbeat.

A tentacle snatched the man off the ground by the ankle and hammered him against the ground head-first. Blood sprayed in a near-perfect circle.

Emanouella pushed off the ground with shaky arms, her movements unrushed. Blood streamed from her head and dripped off her chin, staining her white silk gown.

"Get up," Oskar said, hands curling into fists, his words lost in the chaos. "Get up."

She stood and her blinks came slow and sleepy. The realization of her situation showed when her eyes widened, and her entire body stilled.

Then her shoulders lowered, and her fingers unfurled at her sides. Emanouella faced the serpulagus with her chin lifted.

Stupid, brave woman. It was one thing to dare the market alone at night and to sneak around like a commoner. Standing before a monster with fortitude as her only weapon was quite another.

And he would be damned if she died believing she was alone in this world. That no one cared.

Cursing, Oskar leapt.

The serpulagus blurred in and out of focus, and the ringing in Emanouella's ears might split her head into four. The important thing she gathered was that the beast was engaged elsewhere, removing her from immediate danger. It took every jab of spear, sword, and ax as a man would a needle.

She should run while it was distracted, but it was hard to pull herself out of the heaviness of her body. If she stayed here, it would all be over soon. She wouldn't have to go another day feeling like this—

An arm hooked around her waist and hauled her into a run. It was *him*.

What was he doing here?

A tentacle slammed down on her right, and the man spun her left. Then right again as a second struck.

"Duck!" he shouted.

The air shifted above her head, and she would have fallen forward if not for his steady hold.

"Run," he ordered. "Do not look back."

They bounded up against the bars to the nearest access tunnel. Only a corridor painted by quiet shadows stared back.

He yanked on the metal handle, and his sleeve rose above a brand of a bird in flight and a sword. This wasn't just any man. He was a Blade.

"Fuck," he said. "It's locked."

Words clambered into her throat and lodged with her tears. "You shouldn't have come. You'll only die with me."

He scanned the arena. The serpulagus slithered back into the pool, and once submerged, the creature began its death spiral to collect any swimmers.

"We're not dying today," he said, then pointed to another access door some twenty feet away. "There."

They ran, this time without interference. As they neared their destination, a man's shadow materialized at the second barred entryway.

Emanouella shouted an order ahead of their arrival. "Open the door!"

The man—one of the beastmaster's slaves—shook his head and backed deeper into the hallway. His attention drew a frozen, rigid line to something behind them.

She sensed the hulking creature only seconds before its shadow overtook them.

<hr>

Oskar knew they were dead the moment the shadow cooled his back. His daggers were no better than sticks against those tentacles.

He spun with Emanouella pulled tight against his side, and her arms came up to protect her head.

The tentacle struck the bars right where he'd been standing.

"Run!" He dragged her back into the arena and held her upright as her sandals slid in the damp dirt and gravel.

The serpulagus was half-submerged in the pool, its beady eyes following their futile flight. It crawled right for them, and Oskar could almost feel its furious intent.

Two men armed with spears raced forward, shouting to get the beast's attention. Unlike the slaves forcibly entered into this fight, they weren't outfitted in soldier garb. They were dressed like regular citizens. One wore a brand on his neck: a longsword crossing a bird in flight.

Paschalis and Evangelos.

His brothers.

Blades.

Oskar veered out of the way with Emanoulla's small, fragile hand in his.

A tentacle swept the ground toward the Blades, and they somersaulted overtop with the ease of a god commanding air.

The crowd erupted in cheers. Even with their queen in danger, this was all a part of the games to them.

The remaining survivors hobbled toward the outer walls, bloody and exhausted, skin coated in sweat and dirt. One sobbed on his knees, hands raised in prayer to the gods.

Evangelos halted before the squid, pulled back his spear arm with practiced precision, and threw with his entire body. The spear hurtled through the air—

The weapon struck an eye and stayed there.

The serpulagus roared and retreated, whipping its head about. When the spear didn't fall out, it wrapped a tentacle around the intrusive wood and yanked it free.

Paschalis made to repeat the gesture on the remaining eye—

A tentacle knocked him off his feet and he struck the far wall. Paschalis bounced off and landed on his stomach with a grunt. The crowd cheered as the Blade began to rise, cradling an arm.

Evangelos sprinted by Paschalis, retrieving both his brother and their last spear.

"I think I know a way out," Emanouella said. Her voice was like a siren in the eye of a hurricane, drawing Oskar's full attention. "It's mad, and we may die anyway."

"Tell me." He saw no alternative, especially if the beastmaster's men were too scared to open the gates for them.

She pointed at the pool. "There's a tunnel feeding seawater in from the bay."

Oskar didn't need to hear anything else. If his brothers kept the serpulagus distracted, they could take advantage of what little time they had to escape.

He caught Evangelos's attention and pointed at the pool. "Tunnel."

The Blade nodded. "We'll be right behind you." Then Evangelos called out to the squid with a daring grin. "Over here, you bastard."

Oskar and Emanouella rounded the squid, avoiding its furious tentacles.

At the water's edge, Oskar met her eyes. "You're certain you want to do this?"

"I'd rather drown trying than end up in that thing's stomach."

He grinned. "Right. Deep breath, then, Your Majesty."

3

Emanouella couldn't move suddenly. Seconds ago, the tunnel opening hadn't looked that far away.

The Blade's brows drew together, his attention darting to the serpulagus and back. "If we're doing this, we have to go now."

Her nod quivered. "We're doing this."

"Deep breath on the count of one. One."

Eyes locked, she mirrored his deep breath, then together they dove into the pool. The water felt like ice on her overheated skin. Her skirts twisted around her kicking feet. All at once, she needed more air. Her throat hurt, and black spots filled her vision.

She wasn't going to make it.

The Blade took her around the waist, and even with one arm, he pulled them at twice the rate she would have on her own. She redoubled her efforts, even if her help felt useless.

The tunnel was close, only a few more feet—

The serpulagus plunged into the pool.

Emanouella's heartbeat thrashed in her ears, and the Blade's voice played on repeat. *Don't look back. Don't look back.*

A current appeared where there hadn't been one, not unlike a gentle breeze. The shadow of tentacles blotted out the sunlight on the pool bottom, spreading and turning.

The current pulled with a gentle hand, and then it *tugged*. Their trajectory shifted diagonally.

The Blade tensed, and his strokes became more desperate.

Emanouella kicked and kicked and kicked. Her arms *burned*. The water dragged her feet into the maelstrom as the Blade stretched toward the tunnel lip, fingers strained.

The vortex yanked Emanouella into the spin. She fumbled for his shoulder, then her fingertips slid down his tunic and arm.

His hand grabbed hers so tight that her knuckles rubbed together, and her runaway body yanked to a stop. The Blade's teeth flashed in the water, and he heaved. His other hand held tight to the tunnel lip on his other side.

He helped her to the ledge and pushed her into the much calmer water.

With lungs on fire and muscles aching to stop, Emanouella swam with her final vestiges of strength through the tunnel. The walls and floors dipped deeper but eventually began to rise. All light disappeared, and she let her fingertips scrape the coarse wall sides to guide her up and up and up—

Emanouella burst into a pocket of air and sucked oxygen into her screaming lungs, taking water with it. She coughed at the intrusion and flailed, her entire body revolting. The Blade burst into the dark beside her with a scraping gasp for air. He, too, began coughing.

"Are you all right?" she asked, her tone raspy.

"Inhaled a bit of water," he said around a wracking cough, "but fine. You?"

His fingers grappled for her waist beneath the water, and she allowed him to gather her weight. Exhaustion gripped her in a taut fist. She clung to his round shoulders, and gratitude poured through her and she pulled him into a hug. Their legs interlaced as they treaded water together, and he hugged her back.

"Thank you," she whispered.

The Blade shivered. "Let's get out of here."

Oskar began to fear they'd never get out of the tunnel. The way was pitch dark, and the floor plunged them back into the water on a whim. That wasn't even the worst part. The bay's water had no warmth to it this time of year. Without the heat of sunlight, they were wracked by shivers by the time they erupted like half-dead fish through a chute into Castona Bay.

The queen bobbed low on the rippling surface, her lips blue and breathing shallow. Her face dunked under several times before he gathered her back to his chest. Exhaustion tugged at him, and he had to stop and float often, but he eventually got them to the beach, where they collapsed.

The sodden, cool ground had never felt so good.

Emanouella barely moved to look around. "Do you know where we are?"

He didn't care, but he sat up to see if he recognized the cove. It could have been one of several, but the high bluff walls looked familiar. "I think the palace is that way."

She sat up to follow his pointed finger. Beach sand coated her hair and skin like a gritty layer of clothing.

"We can be there in an hour or so," he said, already dreading the trip.

Her throat bobbed with a deep swallow before she met his eyes. "Do we have to go?"

"Go? Not right away. We can rest for however long you—"

"At all, I mean." Emanouella crawled to his side and took his hand. She was shaking, and he might have thought it was the cold, but something like hope and desperation lit her eyes, which were like the brown of dark honey. "No one knows where I am. I doubt they'll even look for me."

Her lip wobbled, and tears spilled over her lids. She released him from her gaze, and the beach and surf and sky returned to their rightful places. A wave crashed several feet away, and cold water skimmed past them a moment later.

If he knew words at all, he couldn't locate them. His mouth bobbed open just in case he found one. He only needed one, and then the rest would follow.

Emanouella rattled her head and swiped roughly at her tears. "I'm sorry. That was silly of me to even ask."

"Can I at least know why?"

She blew out a breath. "For a moment back there, I was prepared to die. I was okay with it, grateful even, that the end was a breath away." She stared down at her fingers that twisted and smoothed her silk skirts. "I've lost perspective, and if I'm going to be strong for my son, I can't return like this."

Her brown eyes returned to his, and he couldn't look away if he tried. Even pale and shivering, even dotted by sand and waterlogged, that woman was still in there. The one who faced death with her chin high. He didn't care what she said. That had been the purest form of bravery to face death with such confidence.

But he wouldn't dismiss her feelings, either, no matter how it had appeared on the outside. "I will help you however I can, Your Majesty."

A gust of air shot out of her, and she beamed. "Thank you—" She halted, her brows dipped. "I don't know your name."

"Oskar Dahlin."

"Emanouella," she said and gave him a watery smile. "Now we're friends."

He had friends, but none made him so aware of every brush of air across his skin. He still felt the way her waist molded into his palm, and now the emptiness in his hands felt heavy and vast.

Oskar swallowed. "Friends."

In the following days, Emanouella felt possessed by a dark heaviness. Disappearing from her life, even if only temporarily, was insane, and she should return home, but she couldn't bring herself to *want* to. She needed time to process recent events and her role in them. She needed to understand *why* she'd been so ready to die.

Until then, no one needed her. Angelos would be cared for by his governess and protected by his Royal Guard. As for her husband... Honestly, she didn't care what Orestis thought of her absence. Why should she when her presence hadn't mattered until it was time to babysit another man's wife?

So, she took refuge in Oskar's single-story cottage, which stood in mild disrepair. It was surrounded by the ivory forest, shadowed by a dense canopy, and fit perfectly inside a small clearing. The forest had taken to growing up the outer stone walls and chimney. The lanterns on either side of the door had rusted, and the three wooden stairs to the door had warped from the weather.

A stream ran behind the cottage, which was convenient for several reasons. Someone had once cared for a garden in the front— not that it had survived, but another could easily be planted in its place.

It was everything her life wasn't.

It was perfect.

Oskar's home was one open, spacious room that contained the previous occupants' original furniture. A small table near a wood stove and an icebox that needed immediate replacing. Stools before the cold fireplace. The bath was made from the same stone as the floor with only a half-wall for privacy. And there was a bed with a thin cot wide enough for two.

There were personal touches as well. A cloth runner on the table. Cracked pottery for eating and cooking. A chest for linens, bedding, and clothes—still full but moth-eaten. Worn, frayed rugs. Rolls of silk the previous lady of the house, Natalia, would have carted down to the market now sat in ruin.

No one had lived here for many years, Oskar had explained. The home had belonged to a friend and his wife, who had disappeared long ago, and because Oskar had looked withdrawn at the mere mention, Emanouella didn't ask.

From their first day sharing his home, he ensured she had everything she required. Hot water for her bath and fresh clothes to wear afterward. She could have passed for one of her own people without her usual silks and jewelry. Even her hair hung mostly loose to her waist each day or in a singular braid when necessary.

She didn't have to shine with delight or glow from happiness or sparkle with joy. She smiled when it came naturally. She hadn't yet laughed but knew she would when the time was right. And that it would be Oskar who brought her to it.

Much of their days passed in companionable silence as they worked on his home. She hadn't given it a second thought to join him that first day he began cleaning. Without a word, she filled a bucket with fresh water and wiped down surfaces while he swept and discarded any items not worth salvaging.

For the first time in her life, Emanouella learned what it was like to scrub a floor on her knees. She found it meditative work, and when the inside was done, she moved on to the overgrown gardens while Oskar repaired the roof.

Once that was complete, Oskar replaced all the old furniture and added new, vibrant-colored rugs. One day they ate from cracked pottery, and the next he appeared with some that had been newly handmade by local artisans.

After her first full week, things had been mostly uneventful until he burst through the door with an excited gleam in his eyes. He wore Guild black, having just returned from the East Harbor Market. "Come. You have to see this."

They hurried through the forest until they burst into a field flush with color. Blues, reds, yellows, oranges, and greens. The arrangement of wildflowers butted up against a bluff that overlooked Castona Bay.

Emanouella didn't know if she wanted to spin or run or fly first, but her cheeks already hurt from smiling. "This was here the whole time?"

Oskar smiled warmly at the field. "There wasn't much to see before. This is the first I've seen full blooms."

She whisked into the lush, vibrant field, a laugh erupting from her chest. Its wildness inspired her to spin and spin and spin until the colors blurred. Finally, she collapsed to her back, out of breath.

Oskar appeared over her, grinning, hands on his hips. "Are you all right?"

"I'm magnificent." She reached up for his hand. "Lie with me. Look at these clouds, Oskar."

The sky was a perfect azure, and the billowing clouds were pristinely white.

Oskar dutifully did as asked and lay beside her. He squinted at the bright sky. "I've never done this before."

She let her head fall to the side and took in his profile. "That sounds like a complete waste of time not to have."

His eyes crinkled with a smile, and his head fell toward her.

How had she never noticed before now? His eyes were the most unique shade of pale gray, with blue shot through like sunbursts.

Oskar's expression sobered. "There have been other awe-inspiring things to look at."

His pinky slid up against hers.

The entire presence of this man shifted as if a moment ago, he was no more than a comforting daydream. Now, Oskar was a realm of possibilities she had no right to consider. She wanted to trace the outline of his tight beard. She liked how his hair sometimes fell across his forehead and made him look younger. And his body—she'd have to be blind not to have noticed how trim and muscular he was after days working on the house without his shirt.

Oskar was calloused and strong, yet gentle and considerate.

And when he spoke to her like that, his words became sunlight and water, unlocking her from a cold, deep grave. Giving her roots the strength to spread.

"If you keep speaking to me like that," she said, suddenly breathless, "I may never return home."

His gaze tore from her and lifted back to the sky. He cleared his throat. "Apollon Rodelis has announced that he will hold prayers for your crossing to the Valley in two days' time."

This news plunged her into icy water. "They have declared me dead?"

"No one has seen you since you dove into the serpulagus pool."

Emanouella sat up, and the wildflowers blurred for a whole new reason. "Did anyone even bother to *look* for me?"

"Not to my knowledge, no." He sat up and hugged his knees. "To be fair, we survived great odds that day. I might not have believed it myself had I not been there. Without a body, you may as well be in the belly of that beast."

She should have considered this. Not that she'd been thinking clearly. But no one had survived that pit, not even his Guild brothers. There'd been no victor, and it had been absolute chaos in the aftermath of the assassination attempts on the royal platform. Her nephew and the empress from Tineian had been the only casualties. More would have died if not for the Yirian triad.

And now her son believed she was dead. She didn't much care what everyone else thought, but Angelos mattered. He must be devastated.

Emanouella thrust her hands through her windswept hair. "What should I do?"

"You do whatever you want. You're the queen."

"If I decide to sail to lands that have yet to be recorded on our maps?" She was only half-serious. Vanishing from Perean had never been a consideration, and she'd never leave without her son.

Oskar didn't hesitate to respond. "Then I will book your passage."

"Would you think ill of me for leaving?"

He met her gaze, then he stood and reached for her hand. "Come. There's more you should see."

Oskar led her to the bluff's edge where the wind tugged at her loose hair and pasted her skirt to her legs. All of Praevia was visible from here. The palace, the homes, the temple...everything. From this distance, the capital almost looked majestic. Who wouldn't want to live in a city like this?

"I understand hating this place," he said. "It took me a very long time to forgive its wrongs and what it took from me."

She sensed he would finally open up to her, so she risked asking, "What has the city taken from you?"

"My family. Then later, the friend who was the nearest thing to a brother I ever had."

"You had a family?"

He shrugged. "I had parents I never knew. They sold me to the Guild as a young child, which happened to almost all of us. Some people simply can't afford to feed themselves, let alone a child. And this choice gives their children a chance to survive.

"Hristos became my father. The Blades my brothers. They're not a poor replacement by any stretch of the imagination, but sometimes I wonder where my blood comes from."

"Sharing blood with someone doesn't always make a family. Titos Demakis is my brother, but he wouldn't use his body as a shield to protect me. I doubt he's mourning my loss and won't so much as raise an eyebrow when I reappear."

"And your husband?"

Emanouella sighed. "He's likely gathering a list of potential wives as we speak."

"I'm sorry."

"Don't be." She attempted to smile up at him. "You mentioned your lost friend. Is this the one who built the cottage?"

"Nikos Thanides." A sad smile spread, and Oskar strode back through the field. "I was with Nikos when he first found this place.

We walked through the woods for hours before finding the perfect spot for the cottage. He wasn't one for courtyards and lots of rooms, so he kept it simple. Though he talked about eventually adding a second floor for when they had children."

"What about his wife? Did she mind living in a smaller home?"

"Natalia loved him so much that she would have lived on the ground under the stars if that was what he wanted." He smiled faintly as if losing himself to a fond memory. "I've never known anyone to be more in love than they were."

O skar never talked about Nikos and Natalia, not really, and he was mildly surprised that it didn't hurt to do so. Confiding in Emanouella and spending time with her was...

He refused to give it words. The entire week with her had felt more natural than it should. As if they'd known each other their entire lives.

"Thank you for sharing this with me." Emanouella swept a glance at the field. "And now that I've seen it, I believe you owe me an explanation." She picked a blue flower and held it pointedly up to him.

He looked between her and the flower, then heat flashed through his face, neck, and ears. She figured it out.

"It was you, wasn't it? At the temple? Why keep it from me?"

Oskar rubbed the back of his neck. "I didn't want you to think I had intentionally intruded on your private moment. I didn't even know who you were."

She folded her arms. "It was a coincidence? That's what you're telling me?"

"I thought so at first. After everything, I can't help but wonder if the gods had a hand in throwing us together too."

Emanouella's beautiful, full lips turned up on one side. She hadn't smiled this much the entire week, and all he had to do was show her his favorite place in the world.

"I wonder the same thing," she said, lowering her gaze. A pink tinge entered her cheeks, and another of those rare smiles flashed.

Oskar would have closed the gap between them if she'd been any other woman. Every day with her was a struggle. Not only did he find her immensely attractive, he *liked* her. Gods, the woman was boiling over with untapped strength and she had no idea.

She was also a woman who was defeated by her life.

As much as he needed her to return home—before he did something ill-advised—he hoped she'd stay for no other reason than to put herself back together.

"You haven't asked me," she began, squinting to blot out the sharp sun, "why I was in the temple that night. Hiding like a commoner. Why I was upset."

"No. I didn't." He wouldn't ask why but was prepared to listen if she was ready.

Her keen brown eyes, rimmed with the blackest of lashes, shifted away from him. "I lost a child and needed a moment to grieve alone before telling my husband."

Oskar was in front of her, hands on her shoulders before he realized he'd thought to move. "I'm so sorry."

Tears glistened in her eyes. "Thank you."

"Is there anything you need—?"

"You've already done it, Oskar. You let me into your home and gave me the space to begin healing. I can't tell you what that means to me." Her hand came up to rest over his heart. "I wish…"

Emanouella stepped away and rattled her head. The smile she flashed wasn't at all like the others. This one was forced. Still beautiful, but it lacked her essence.

"I'll leave soon," she said. "I've overstayed—"

"You haven't."

She took a moment to decide if that was true, then said, "Promise me something."

He nodded. He'd give her anything she asked for.

"When I return to the palace, I'd feel better knowing that I have an ally out here in the world. Even if I don't get to see you every day."

Oskar let a smile surface. "You cleaned my floors on your hands and knees. You're stuck with me for the rest of your life."

She beamed. "Then I think I'm ready."

4

Emanouella held the dried and pressed flower to her nose and was almost immediately transported out of her sitting room and into Oskar's field. Days after returning, much of them spent telling lies and shedding tears, she could still clearly see him that last day. Considerate and patient. Handsome. It had been a long time since her stomach fluttered in reaction to a man's smile. Better still, he never once treated her like royalty. He let her get dirty and didn't try to stop her.

"You cleaned my floors on your hands and knees. You're stuck with me for the rest of your life."

A laugh filled with both joy and sadness rippled from her. He'd been making light of her request for a friend, but she hadn't doubted his sincerity. He'd be there if and when she ever needed him. He couldn't possibly know what that meant to her.

She was on her balcony, staring up at Oskar's bluff, when her husband's hands, calloused from daily combat practice, fell on her shoulders, and his body warmed her back.

He kissed her cheek. "Good morning."

Emanouella became a vortex of sensations, her stomach sinking toward her knees and her heart leaping toward her throat before they snapped back like released rubber. Trapped inside this whirlwind, she released the blue flower over the marble banister.

She turned and smiled. "Good morning, husband."

Orestis's fingertips brushed ever-so-softly across her cheek. "You're looking a little flushed. Are you all right?"

What was she supposed to do with these flashes of warmth passing through his icy blue eyes? It wasn't him, or hadn't been before she "died." Was she supposed to believe he suddenly appreciated her? After eight years?

She took a half-step back and shifted her chin to the side. "I'm perfectly fine."

His jaw muscles flared toward his ears. "The healer said you're well after the ordeal."

He didn't mean the escape from the arena, but the miscarriage. The one good thing to come out of that attack was that she had somewhere to place the blame. The result had surprised her. Orestis had expressed...remorse.

"I will need a few more weeks," she said. "But overall, I am much better."

Orestis tucked hair behind her ear, and for a moment, he was her handsome husband: thick, blond waves of hair that sometimes fell over his forehead and the hint of a cleft in his chin. He had a look of gentle kindness about him, though it was nothing more than a mask.

Guilt sat heavy in her chest.

She hadn't wanted to love, or be loved, by her husband in years. Not until another filled her every waking thought. She wished things could have been different.

"Have breakfast with me," Orestis said.

Emanouella gave him what she hoped was an apology in her smile. "I promised the morning to Angelos."

His mask began slipping. "You've spent every morning with him since you returned."

"He thought I had died, and it broke his heart. Is it so wrong that I want to make it up to him?"

"I thought you were dead too. I don't see you making it up to me."

A slap wouldn't have been nearly as effective as his cutting words. And even though it made her sick, she said, "What can I do?"

Orestis gripped the banister. He glared at the world unfolding in the muted hues of the morning as if the fresh air and the sounds of the crashing surf offended him.

Emanouella resisted the urge to touch him. She didn't want him to see it as an opening to be touched in return.

He sighed and pushed upright. "It's time Angelos begins to spend his time elsewhere."

Her heart skipped. "What does that mean?"

"He's going to be king one day, and it's my job to ensure he's prepared."

"He's *five*."

"The men of the Tineian Empire begin military training at his age. All families send their sons away to train; by sixteen, they are fully active in the military. The Tineians have the greatest military force in the world. And what does Perean have? A decent Horse Guard? We barely have a proper naval fleet, and we control three times more waterfront than Soterra."

Emanouella wanted to scream, *So do something about it*, but didn't dare. Instead, she said, "Would you rather our son grow to be a great military leader and think us strangers? My father once said that a man who learns compassion at an early age makes for a greater king to his people."

A fresh storm waged in her husband's eyes. "And what would your father say about me, considering my upbringing included neither of those?"

"I wouldn't presume to know."

A lie. Her father worried that Orestis had too much ambition. That her husband was overly concerned with what the world thought of him. That combination would only lead to grave mistakes.

"Orestis, please," she begged, taking his hand. "Let our son be a child for a little while longer. That's all I ask."

He shook his head and started off the balcony. "I have matters to attend to."

Chrysanthi appeared just as he reentered the apartments and dropped into a bow that he ignored.

Emanouella shook off her tension. "Good morning."

"Good morning, Your Majesty." She handed over a sealed fold of parchment. "This just arrived for you."

"Thank you."

With her mind half-gone on her husband's departure and his potential plans, she broke the unfamiliar wax seal.

A flattened wildflower—the color of burnt orange—fell to her feet.

"Who's that from?" the handmaid asked.

The parchment was blank, but Emanuella didn't need any words. She retrieved the flower and smiled. "A friend."

<hr>

The sun rose for the second time like a rebirth. The world had been cold and gray, and now the air was fragrant with fruit and the cosmos rife with color. Taste, sound, sight. Life.

Oskar blinked the blur from his eyes and came alive for the first time in days.

Emanouella wound through the market as if she believed the lie of her outfit. As if she truly were a poor beggar woman in a worn chiton the color of an old, used-up bronze coin. The loose fit brought attention to her protruding collarbone and thin frame.

What did she think she was doing out here all alone?

He knew she liked slipping out at night in commoner garb, but it was midday, and half the capital was gathered outside the temple.

He knew why *he* was here. The City Guard loved these sorts of crowds. Where the more destitute congregated at the steps for a monthly handout of food and clothes. The line stretched from the temple doors for a full mile.

Emanouella approached the line but remained on the outskirts. Then, she spotted a group of young children playing nearby. She knelt with them, her smile like an invading, hearty root with a fully-fledged flower.

The children engaged with her, laughing and rapt, and then she filled their palms with loose coin. Their delighted squeals could be heard from all over and drew the attention of at least one of the guards.

Oskar darted from his hiding place and swept her out of their range. "That's a good way to get robbed."

She shrugged. "They need it more than me. It's fine."

"I'm not talking about the poor. I'm talking about the City Guard."

Her easy expression vanished. "Oh. I hadn't thought of that."

"What are you doing here?"

Her brown eyes lifted with her soft smile. "Hoping to see a friend."

His heart took flight, and his fingers took on a mind of their own, smoothing her disheveled hair. "Let's get out of here."

"All right, but first, can we...?" She shook her skirts and rattled a bunch of coins.

"How much do you have in there?"

"A lot." She bit her lower lip as the corners of her mouth lifted. "Little help?"

With a smile and a shake of the head, he said, "Stay close. We're going to be moving fast."

<hr>

Over the next few weeks, Oskar's days and nights passed much the same way. Early in their friendship, he let days go by before he caved to the need to hear her voice. And like that first time, he'd send a flower through his palace contacts—no message but the one she'd understand.

Then, hours, sometimes a full day later, she'd appear on his doorstep dressed in common clothes. Shed of everything that made her a queen: poise, courtesy, obligation, and rules.

"Does no one ever notice your absence?" he asked one night. It was late—nearing midnight—and they sat atop a sizable tree trunk that had fallen across the stream.

Emanouella paddled her bare feet in the water, her toes trying to catch every sparkle of moonlight that swam by. "No."

Said as if without the weight of disappointment, but he knew better than to think her impervious. So, he held her hand and hoped she understood that he felt her absence every day.

Another day, shoulder to shoulder in his garden, with the sun directly overhead, she asked, "Have you ever been married?"

"No."

"In love?"

His heart skipped, but he shook his head. "No."

Emanouella sat back on her heels. "Do you want to be?"

Things were getting tricky between them, and he had to be careful. He kept his gaze trained on the tilled dirt in front of him. "Someday."

She returned to the hole she was widening for a bulb. "Me too. Someday."

The resulting thoughts from that response kept him up at night. He'd never considered...

It seemed obvious now. Their marriage had been arranged, and there were plenty of credible rumors about the number of women filling the king's bed.

Then, in midsummer, Emanouella lay in the dense grass with him so they could watch the clouds race by ahead of a storm. She was absent her usual glow. Shared no smile. Her gaze bounced past every detail she normally cherished.

She rarely brought her problems with her, and she never spoke openly about her marriage, but something must have happened.

Oskar held his hands atop his stomach, watched the sky, and waited. She wasn't unlike the tension building in the air around them in preparation for the rain.

"Sometimes," she began in a soft voice, "I lay in bed and wonder what's beyond our maps. Do you think anyone's ever looked?"

"I can't imagine no one's tried."

"This can't be all there is." This time, her words came strained. Something was really wrong.

Oskar rolled to his side and propped onto his elbow. "Has something happened?"

A tear escaped the corner of her eye and rolled into her ear. "The blooms are fading. Soon, autumn will arrive, and they'll all be gone."

True panic seized him. "Em?"

Her eyes shut. "You'll keep your promise, won't you? To be my friend and ally? To be the one person I can turn to? No matter what?"

"What's going on?"

"Duty and expectations."

Understanding fell upon him like an anvil, and a boulder lodged in his throat. Oskar's duties were to the people of this city.

Hers was to a marriage bed.

A raincloud burst overhead, and Emanouella went with it. Oskar pulled her into him and held on as she released everything she'd pent up onto his chest.

Some weeks later, as the blooms did indeed begin to fade around them, Emanouella huddled beneath his arm. They sat as near to the bluff as they dared, watching the sunset. The sea was a perfect shade of cerulean, and the sky darkened with layers of deepest red to the palest orange.

"If you could do anything in the world," Oskar began, "what would you do?"

She peered up at him and smiled. "That's easy. I would be the sort of queen that would have made my parents proud. My father raised me inside council chambers and by this throne. I learned to rule as well as Titos. We all did. My father listened to my mother's council, and they were loved by the Sotteran people."

Emanouella straightened out of his arms and twisted to face him. "I would choose to be just as useful to the people of Perean rather than the shell of a woman with an important title. And…"

Her gaze drifted to his mouth, and the mere inches between them were no better than a door that had been blasted open.

"And?" he dared to ask, heart pounding.

"And…" Emanouella met his gaze. "I would choose a man for love. Not for power or political gain." Her fingers crossed that barrier, hesitant and alarmingly slow, and pushed the hair off his brow. Her next words came as a whisper. "I would choose you."

For just a moment, Oskar marveled at how easily contentment flowed directly from her into him. How her trust was so easily shared. Being this near was a constant battle against his basest instincts to inhale her. Strip her to her bare skin. Taste and devour and plunge.

And she wanted him.

Him.

An idea he'd refused to consider because how could this precious creature, nurtured by power and greed and obligation, dare to accept him? A man hardened by hunger and benevolence and the freedom of choice.

A man with the blood of power and greed and obligation all over his hands.

Emanouella's fingertips trailed down his temple and cheek. Her throat bobbed, and she inched forward. A tremble went through her.

Oskar cupped her cheek and brought his face to hers. He couldn't kiss her—not yet. The battle between what was right and what was wrong waged through him. Because—gods help him—he loved this woman. And she could never truly be his. Powerful men and the law decided that for him long ago.

But, he could be hers. Maybe that was enough.

Their noses skimmed and circled, and their breath mingled. He could almost taste her.

He gritted his teeth. "Em."

She gripped the back of his neck and pushed fingers up into his hair. "It's all right," she whispered. She was a siren, and this was her song.

Oskar gave himself over to her.

Their lips met and, at first, he couldn't move. It was disbelief—*surely this was a dream*—that stayed him.

Then her mouth eased open, and he fulfilled all those dreams that had been plaguing him for months. He tasted her tongue as he pulled her onto his lap. Straddling him, her entire body curled around him. Her spine arched with his climbing palms, and her hips rolled deeper into his lap.

They touched anywhere and everywhere, and it was desperation for more that had him spinning her onto her back. Their kiss barely broke, and she moaned as he used this new angle to leverage his tongue deeper inside. He pressed his aching cock into her—it wasn't the relief he thought it'd be. He needed more and more and—

Stop.

They had to stop.

"Don't stop," she said, clutching his face. Her gaze latched onto his and refused to let go. "Make love to me. Here amongst the flowers. With the gods above as our witness."

And because he would never deny her anything, he did.

5

Two Years Later

Emanouella raced toward the shouts and screams, well ahead of her Queen's Guard.

This was a part of the city no one talked about. The adults looked half-starved, and likely were. The children sat half-dressed in mud and reeking of the foulest of odors.

She had to block it out or she'd never make it in time.

They await a marriage of enemies...

Such an innocuous collection of words that anyone could easily dismiss. She had. Once.

Now, she understood that the gods had intended for her to marry Orestis. Their betrothal brought two enemy nations together, and her marriage maintained their fragile peace. This accord allowed Orestis unfettered access to the volcanic mountain inside the Soterran border.

And it was her failure, her refusal to believe, that led to two innocent deaths nine months ago.

It was her husband who—

She ground her teeth together. Never again. She wouldn't allow it.

Chaos filled the cobbled streets around the family's home. News of the birth had given the locals something to feast on, and the City Guard descended like vultures. It had been like this for weeks and would continue until the second child was located. If at all.

Emanouella ran up against the thick of the crowd with her entire body. "Let me pass," she ordered, sheltering her stomach.

Her Queen's Guard stepped in like a wall of metal and leather, all sharp edges. "Make way for the queen!"

The people moved aside and bowed. A collection of whispers surrounded her.

The scene on the other side added fresh flames to her outrage. Armed soldiers passed a swaddled baby carelessly to the king. A young woman, even younger than Emanouella, sobbed from her knees, still covered in the blood from childbirth.

"Take the child," Orestis said, passing the baby to one of Apollon's acolytes. He hadn't yet noticed her arrival. "Kill the mother."

"Don't you dare!" Emanouella yelled.

Orestis stiffened, the perfect model for the statue of his likeness in the harbor. The mold broke a moment later, and he stormed over. He seized her by the arm, eyes blazing. "What are you doing here?" His attention fell briefly to the swell of her belly. The only thing he cared about between them.

She met his grit with her own. "Release me."

"Or what?"

"Is my brother aware of the Perean scholars practically living inside a mountain on his side of the border? And that you've installed a *cage* for your own nefarious purposes?" She pressed closer and held his gaze. "He might do something about that, don't you think? Maybe even destroy the entrance."

His lips flattened, and he stepped away.

Emanouella motioned the acolyte over. "Give me the child."

The baby was so fresh and new. Eyes still shut to the world, sleeping through everything.

"My Lady," the woman sobbed, "help my daughter. Please."

Emanouella looked from her to the king. "What crime could this woman have possibly committed within only hours of giving birth?"

"Her husband attacked my men." Orestis glanced into the hovel where a man with blond hair lay in a pool of his own blood.

"He was only protecting our child," the woman said.

This poor family. They'd fallen into a trap laid by the gods themselves, and the king was the monster who would kill anyone in his way.

"The palace kitchen has a shortage of cooks," Emanouella said. "She can fulfill her husband's debt in service to the crown. The child too. Two lives for one should appease your disgruntled gods."

She hated herself in that moment, making this woman a slave. The alternative, however, was far worse.

Orestis dragged her out of earshot. "I have cast my judgment."

"I would hate for something tragic to befall this child." It was the one threat she could make that would ruin all his plans, even if he were ever to find the boy. She cupped the girl's head. "Babies have such fragile necks."

His eyes narrowed. "You wouldn't dare."

She wouldn't. Of course, she wouldn't. But she'd say anything to buy time. Only an hour ago, she'd heard of the boy's birth and raced ahead of the news to protect him. His parents lived in very different circumstances, it turned out, and they had a ship at the ready. As long as Emanouella kept Orestis distracted here, he'd never think to look in their direction.

Emanouella motioned for her men to take the woman into their custody, then followed them away from the scene with the baby close to her chest.

"Who are you really doing this for?" Orestis asked. "Him?"

"No." Emanouella looked down at the child in her arms. The

baby's eyelids pried open into slits, one brown eye and one blue peered out. "I'm doing it for her."

PART TWO

A DANDELION IN THE WIND

6

Nineteen Years Later

They cast her son to the sea with a quiet so still they could all hear the lapping of water against the rocks. His body had been wrapped in cloth and ringed in winter garland. Such a peaceful, pretty lie. No one could tell the truth of his mortal state.

Emanouella, however, still felt the weight of his head in her hands. Like when he'd been newly born; light and fragile. Distantly, she'd known that was blood dripping past her wrists to her elbows, but she could only wonder at the color of his skin. He'd never been a very pale boy, so this couldn't be him.

Not her son.

Not her kind, sweet, compassionate Angelos.

Gray, cold, the fear and shock frozen in his lifeless eyes.

A woman's distant sob brought Emanouella back to the sailing before she remembered seeing the remains of Dimos and Faidon as well. And later, the body of their mother Yeorgia, who'd leapt to her death in her overwhelming grief.

The fire-lit arrow arced from the shore to where her son's body floated several feet out, and Angelos's body caught flame.

Her stomach twisted into a tight knot.

No. She couldn't keep doing this. She'd had enough. It'd been enough after the first three pyres were lit. Standing for her lost loved ones, waiting for the burn to sink their vessel. Depositing their ash remains into the sea. But to witness the same for Angelos?

It was too much.

Emanouella turned to leave, but Apollon Rodelis caught her elbow. "Where are you going? This is your son's sailing. You should see his soul off to the Valley."

What did she care for how this looked? What could possibly be so important that he'd force her to watch her only son's body burn? Hadn't she been punished enough?

Emanouella stared at his aging, arthritic hand, then dragged her gaze up his arm until she reached his eyes. "Take your hand off me before I have it cut from your body."

And she would. She'd even enjoy it.

"Leave her be, Apollon," Orestis said, coming up on her side.

Apollon paused only a moment, then bowed to his king. "As you wish."

When she was alone with her husband, she said, "Even today... You can't call him off for one day?"

"I just did, didn't I?" He caressed her arm and frowned. "You don't have to go through this alone."

"Why not? I do everything else alone. You made certain of that."

His shoulders fell toward the rocky ground beneath their feet, and he shook his head.

Time hadn't been kind to her husband, who was now beyond fifty. His once thick blond hair was cut short and almost entirely gray. Age lined his face, and his skin sagged where his once prominent jawline had been. An old riding injury to his back made it hard for him to stand for long periods at a time, though he never let on.

But she noticed.

And she hoped the pain was unbearable.

"Alexandra," Orestis said, turning toward their daughter. "Go with the queen. See that she's taken care of."

The princess came forward, her fine black silks catching the wind like a sail. "Of course, Father. Come, Mother."

Alexandra linked their arms, and they strolled over the embankment toward the palace.

Emanouella pulled her daughter close to kiss her temple. "I thank the gods for you every day."

The princess smiled, and her beauty overshadowed her red-rimmed eyes, the same shade of brown as Emanouella's. Alexandra was an almost exact replica of the young woman Emanouella had been more than two decades ago. With one major difference: Emanouella had already been a mother at her age, and Alexandra continued to enjoy all the freedom one of her status could reasonably have.

"Are you going to be all right, Mother?"

"I don't believe so, my darling. Not for a long time."

Alexandra slowed them to a stop. "What can I do?"

If only her daughter had the power to reverse time. Return her to mornings filled with hope and nights full of dreams.

Emanouella stroked her daughter's cheek. "Be patient with me."

A tiny flare of heat caught in Alexandra's eyes. "Nothing this deplorable will ever happen to those I love when I'm Queen."

Emanouella flinched as her words took root, and the truth of their situation struck like lightning.

Alexandra would one day rule Perean.

Angelos, the man she'd shaped into her father's image despite Orestis's influence, was truly gone.

Alexandra hadn't been as receptive to Emanouella's teachings. She'd always favored her father, and it showed more and more as time went on. Emanouella loved her daughter but wasn't blind to how cruel she could be. She was more like Orestis than Angelos ever was.

Emanouella squeezed her daughter's hand. "I think I'd like to be alone. You can return to your father."

"Are you sure?"

Her nod wobbled, but Alexandra accepted it and walked away.

Emanouella turned her gaze high to the distant bluff, then went in search of a horse.

The fresh horse droppings on the trail alerted Oskar to his guest, so it wasn't a surprise to find the horse tied to the post in front. He examined the saddle for clues, and his stomach sank.

She wouldn't.

Nothing—*nothing*—in more than twenty years had given her cause to break her promise to stay out of his life. He'd given her the same respect, although he'd made her a different promise once and never broke it. Whether she realized it or not, he'd never stopped being her ally and friend. Even if that meant he could only watch her grow into an incredible queen from afar.

His cottage stood empty, and the stream's embankment remained barren, leaving only one place she would go.

With his heart climbing up his throat, Oskar ventured toward the bluff. He stopped on the outskirts of the field that was nothing more than a sea of half-dead grass. The day was cold, but the wind blew harshly across the elevated terrain and cut like ice.

Emanouella knelt near the edge in her silk finery, staring out to sea. Her hair tangled and whipped around her head, coming loose from intricate twists and the jewels that once held them in place.

Hours ago, she hadn't known that he had stood this close to her, honoring the lost lives with her. He'd felt compelled to be there, even if she'd had no idea. Considering the distant way she'd endured it all, dry-eyed and blank-faced, she hadn't noticed anyone was there.

Oskar retraced her route through newly flattened grass and remembered another time he'd found her waiting for him.

"Come," she said, reaching for his hand, wearing that smile she reserved for only him. "Lie with me and hide from the world."

What young and hopeful fools they'd once been.

Nothing like the woman he approached now. Her body shivered from the cold, but she was utterly frozen otherwise. The sleeves of her dress were slit open from gold cuff to shoulder, revealing goose-flesh along her bare arms. A thoughtless design for this time of year.

He was seconds from admonishing her for not wearing a cloak when she spoke. "There are no flowers." She passed a hand through the tall, stiff blades of grass. "I thought there'd be flowers."

Oskar removed his black cloak and wrapped it around her shoulders, fresh tension tightening his body. Once upon a time, he'd known her better than anyone in the world. He'd been there for some of her worst moments of sadness. And yet, he'd never heard her sound so withdrawn and dispassionate before.

"Winter has begun," he said. "The blooms vanished weeks ago."

"They're always here in my memory."

Oskar knelt, resisting the old urge to touch her. He was surprised, actually, that the urge still existed. Even more surprised that twenty years hadn't transformed her. Yes, the signs of aging were there, but the woman he once loved—her essence—remained. The life he feared would erase her hadn't.

"Why have you come?" he asked, but not harshly. She had always been welcome to return; she'd just chosen not to.

"I needed to feel something else, and I thought—" Her gaze found him suddenly, and a rush of tears sprang from her eyes. "Oskar, they took him from me. My baby boy. I—" She stared into her open palms. "I held him in my hands. His blood is on my hands."

Oskar didn't care about the years between them. He only cared that she was hurting and he couldn't stand it. He pulled her into his arms and begged the gods to take this tragic memory from her. To save her from its constant resurgence.

"What do you need?" he asked when her tears slowed.

Emanouella pulled away, and her eyes blazed. "I need to know who did this."

"Consider it done."

In the dream, Emanouella chased a five-year-old Angelos through her garden, his little laugh carrying into the summer air in pealing squeals and shrieks. She smiled and kept her pace slow as he shouted, "You can't catch me!" over and over again.

Her handmaid interrupted their game, holding a folded piece of parchment. "Your Majesty, this just arrived for you."

The small, sealed missive made her heart race with a new beat. "Thank you, Chrysanthi."

Alone, she cracked the seal, and a dried, pressed flower fell out.

Emanouella startled awake and the room wasn't as it should be. The collage of familiar items came together, pieced together by old, fond memories. Across the room, Oskar knelt to stoke the fire with his back to her. Nothing had changed in the broad line or strength of his shoulders.

For days, she'd awoken to her cold room with the weight of four lost souls upon her. Now, she stretched into the warm sheets and recalled a time when Oskar knelt just where he was, stoking a fire. When she'd been free to say his name, then it would be his weight on her. His hands memorizing her skin. His mouth teasing hers open.

For a moment, she lingered in the past, when her son was alive, and Oskar loved her like no one ever would or had since. She'd regret the deception later, but for now, it didn't matter.

Oskar twisted around, and his expression remained carefully blank. "You're awake."

Emanouella sat on the edge of his cot, her reality returning in painful increments. Her black silk chiton was rumpled, and she must look a disheveled mess. Worse, however, was the way she'd intruded on Oskar's life again.

She hadn't intended for him to find her earlier, though she hadn't gone out of her way to hide. Grief had turned her thoughtless. Still, Oskar deserved better after everything.

"I'm so sorry," she said and stood. "I—"

"Are you hungry?" Oskar crossed the room and began gathering items from his food stores. "I'm starving."

"Oskar, you don't have to—"

"Em, come sit. Eat. Then we should talk."

The old pet name wrapped her like a warm caress and stripped her of all power. She cleaned up, and then they ate in relative silence. Despite their familiarity, the decades apart were no better than spears jammed in the ground, sharp points aimed in either direction. One wrong move and someone would bleed.

But afterward, Oskar put her in front of the fire with the blanket that had once been her favorite. He sat in the second chair beside her, just as he used to, and an old, intimate contentment filled the room. Once, she'd have spent this quiet time dreaming of a future for them that she knew they couldn't have.

"I've missed this," she said, staring at the crackling logs. "Is that all right to say?"

The pause before his answer was a boulder deep in her chest. "You're free to say whatever you like."

"That doesn't make it fair, does it?"

"No."

Sighing, she thrust her fingers through her hair. "Today was… I was going home, but then I looked up at your bluff. This was where I last felt like myself, and the thought of returning to the palace… I needed to be somewhere that had nothing to do with them."

Her son and grandsons. Their little laughs had always reminded her of when Angelos had been that young, carefree, and joyful. Those memories now haunted the palace. Every day felt like a nightmare she couldn't wake from.

"I understand," Oskar said. "I'm glad you felt comfortable enough to come."

"I must have looked a little mad when you found me like that."

A smile twitched. "Not at all."

In profile, Oskar hadn't changed much. More lines fanned from his eyes, and he was grayer. And though he was the same age as her husband, he hadn't aged quite as harshly. Oskar had never been one to let emotions or difficulties get the better of him. His control had always been enviable, and she once attributed this to the sense of peace that lived and breathed in his aura. Clearly, this had benefited him as he aged as well.

The scars through his brow and along his jaw, however? The wounds had been red and raised the last time she saw them, and in the years since, she hadn't considered they'd have done permanent damage. They were just one more thing to add to her mounting guilt.

Oskar's gaze swung toward her, then quickly back to the fire. Clearing his throat, he pitched forward and braced on his knees. "Will anyone know to look for you here?"

"Some secrets remain my own." Nothing Apollon could have ever threatened her with would have made her reveal Oskar's home.

"Where will they think you've gone?"

"I don't know." Nothing about her life had been done in secret in twenty years. She didn't even sneak out at night anymore. "Honestly, I don't care."

It seemed silly now to go on with the same concerns she'd had an entire lifetime ago.

"Good. Because if I'm going to work on locating the person or persons responsible for the deaths, we need to be able to communicate."

Her throat tightened, and she could only nod. "Thank you, Oskar."

"You don't need to thank me. I owe you."

Emanouella froze. "You don't—"

"I know it was you." He glanced over. "The uniform. The time and location. You gave me everything I needed in the end."

"They still died."

"They came back."

A harsh laugh jumped from her chest. "Did that help Selene? She's trapped in the palace with the very man who plots her death. She'll never be free."

"She's alive and will remain so unless her mate appears suddenly. Let's hope he doesn't."

A memory Emanouella hadn't recalled in years flashed by. The young woman with black hair and black eyes, and the handsome man at her side prepared to cut down anyone who got in their way.

"I fear the gods will still find a way to urge him back here," Emanouella *said to the woman.*

Cassia Rutiliana ground her teeth and shook her head. "We'll take him far. He won't so much as see these waters in his lifetime. The gods can't have him."

Emanouella prayed she was right.

To Oskar, she said, "Twenty years later, and we're still fighting the same battle."

Some days, she felt like the battlefield.

"The only thing that matters—that ever mattered—is that we're not fighting each other." His eyes sought hers, the same soft gray with sunbursts of pale blue. "I'm always on your side. You know that, don't you?"

She couldn't get her voice past her tight throat and burst into tears.

Twenty-One Years Ago

Oskar recognized Emanouella's gait from afar, and the weight in his chest immediately lightened. Cloaked and dressed down, she blended in with the commoners strolling the late evening streets.

He walked atop the stone wall that portioned off the cobbled street from a private courtyard. Only the horses sensed his presence and rustled nervously in their stalls.

"Come down from there. Let us speak."

There, in the middle of the street, stood Hristos. All lightness in his mood vanished, replaced by a tightening in his chest. Why was he here? Had something happened?

Oskar leapt down to face his mentor. "Is everything all right?"

"Do you know what you're doing?" This wasn't his usual tone offering wisdom or guidance. This was worry. Anger, even. "You said you would let this go."

Oskar battled with what to say. Telling Hristos that he was fine or there was no reason for concern was exactly the sort of thing he'd have said nine years ago, and Hristos wouldn't believe it.

Hristos grabbed Oskar by the back of the neck and brought their faces close together. "Leave the queen alone. She's innocent of whatever crimes you believe the king is capable of. Gods, he will have your head for this."

He thought Oskar was *using* Emanouella? "You've got this all wrong."

"Do I? I didn't watch you send her a message to the palace through our contacts? I didn't just see her heading this way?"

"My time with Emanouella has nothing to do with my looking into the king and his priest."

"Looking into Nikos's disappearance, you mean."

"I meant what I said. It may connect to Nikos, but it may not."

Hristos stood back and gave a slow, assessing nod, his frown deepening. "When you returned home from Linesh, you swore to me that you were done with this."

"When I came home, I told you that if the gods wanted me to learn the truth, they'd make sure I had it. I can't unlearn what I know, especially when it affects one of the lives we're mandated to protect."

"What are you talking about? Who's life?"

Oskar didn't even know where to begin. Emanouella mentioned the girl inside the temple days ago, not realizing that the offhand remark about blue and brown eyes meant something. Unbeknownst to her, Oskar had seen that rare eye affliction before, and it had greater implications than even he realized before now.

"Her name is Aura Pipidi," Oskar said. "She's one of Apollon's acolytes." Oskar held up a hand to Hristos's incoming interruption. "Go to the temple and see for yourself. Look at her eyes. If you don't immediately know why I'm questioning Apollon's motives, then I'll drop it."

"Just like that?"

"On my honor."

Emanouella strode past the alley, unaware that she'd been spotted.

Hristos shook his head and blew out a harsh breath. "We'll discuss this further later, but end that relationship—for your good and hers. This won't end well for either of you."

Oskar couldn't voice a response. How did he tell the man who was the nearest thing to a father he'd ever known that he'd sooner cut out his own heart?

Emanouella knew whose hand ringed her wrist and brought her into the arched entryway of someone's courtyard. Inside the deep shadows, she gave over to Oskar's mouth on hers. Arched into his strong body and tingled at the feel of his hands stroking her waist and back.

A ravenous heat flashed low in her belly, a dangerous feeling. She had only to lift her skirts and open his trousers, and they could be even closer. It would be so easy.

Oskar moaned and pulled his mouth off hers. He stroked a thumb across her cheek, and his eyes blotted out the darkness and chaos of her life. If the gods were good, she could carry this feeling with her into the coming days, and nothing, not even her husband, could erase it.

His attention fell on her mouth like a soft touch, and she smiled.

Emanouella laid her palm over his drumming, quickened heartbeat, and his hand came overtop hers—

Oskar pulled back abruptly and raised her hand between them. Her wedding ring, the blue and silver of Perean, wielded a sinister kind of magic that broke the spell they were under.

She'd forgotten to take it off. Never, in all these months, had she done that.

His weight fell onto his back foot. "Hristos was right. We're fools to let this continue."

The acceleration of her heart spurred her forward. "Don't say that. *Please* don't say that." Emanouella fisted his tunic. "I think I..." She swallowed the stone in her throat. "Is this not love we feel for one another?"

Oskar's expression crumbled. "What does it matter? You are *the queen.*"

"I don't have to be." She'd finally said the words aloud. For weeks, she'd kept those thoughts to herself, allowing common sense and logic to stomp all over every word. Now, however, she didn't dare let rational thought play into anything she said next. "Who would stop us from taking a ship to somewhere—*anywhere*? We could sail to lands beyond our maps and change our names and our entire histories."

"What about your son?" His tone mocked, and he folded his arms.

She wouldn't let him dissuade her. "Angelos will come with us.

Orestis can remarry a woman who can give him more children than he can count. It's not too late for *any* of us to have the life we desire."

She'd faked her death once—by accident, yes—and no one had questioned it. Maybe she could devise a similar situation—controlled this time—for herself and Angelos. They could disappear, and no one would think of looking for them.

Oskar's gentle hold on her face halted her plotting. "Don't look at me like that. You know how hard it is for me to deny you anything."

"Why would you deny me this? Deny *us*?"

Head shaking, he turned away from her. "The temple acolyte, Aura."

"What about her?" Then, it struck her like a punch. "Are you with her?"

"No! No. Gods, no." He returned and took her hands. "Em, *I'm with you*. But there are things I haven't told you about Apollon and Orestis and... You'll think me mad when I tell you."

"You must think very little of me if you believe that." She'd never known anyone whose words she could trust more.

A wagon wheeled by, followed closely by a couple laughing and whispering and stumbling. Drunk, most likely. Returning home from some tavern.

"We should go somewhere else," Oskar suggested, and he took her by the hand. Then, as if possessed, he stopped and kissed her fingertips one by one. "You love me?"

How could he ask that? How could he seek an answer when he was, at present, attempting to place distance between them? "Will you still leave me after I tell you that I will follow you to the ends of the earth for the rest of my days?"

He shook his head and placed a kiss on her open palm. "No, because I would follow you into death, Emanouella."

Heat sprang to her eyes. "Oskar."

Oskar raised her chin and kissed her tenderly. "May the gods help us, but I love you as well."

7

Present Day

They spent all their time outdoors during the following weeks, though winter was now truly upon them. When Emanouella occasionally arrived on his doorstep, she came draped in the thickest furs and fabrics. Her boots crunched on the patches of snow dotting the forest floor, and she appeared unbothered by the cold.

Oskar imagined she had greater concerns to deal with than personal comfort. They still didn't know who'd murdered her family or why.

"The Otuvians?" she suggested during one such walk.

They'd been the first place he'd looked. Twenty-two years ago, the Otuvians who attacked the royals during the games had been a rogue band. The one man King Vidalaotos kept alive for questioning admitted they'd acted on behalf of—not directly for—Quintus Gregorius, the man who'd once been Otuvia's king.

Quintus had been forced to re-pledge his fealty to Orestis and Titos on bended knee, swearing against these acts of violence.

To this day, Oskar wondered if Quintus truly meant it. He'd lost his throne and his wealth during a war that had completely blind-sided him. For a man who, by all accounts, assassinated two crown princes, one would think he'd have prepared for such action.

"The Otuvians have been quiet," Oskar said. "I've heard no whispers as to the possibility."

She sighed. "Neither has Orestis's men, but they're useless. I don't think they care."

Likely because Angelos was his father's opposite. From what Oskar had seen, Angelos had been a lot like Emanouella. Discreetly strong. Open to change. He saw the people, not the power. The young man had been loved, and many had eagerly anticipated the day he'd be crowned.

Oskar didn't get the same sense regarding Alexandra, however. She was something else entirely. He couldn't quite put his finger on what, though.

He should look at the King's Council. Was someone intentionally ensuring their future monarch to protect their seat? It was entirely possible.

"Could my brother Titos have done this?" Emanouella asked, sitting on a fallen tree trunk. She wrapped her thick gray cloak tighter around her and closed her eyes to the even grayer sky. The day was bright but subdued in a way one only saw during these cold months.

When had she last slept? Dark circles ringed her eyes, and her skin was more pallid than usual.

Oskar debated asking. There was a time he would have, but things were different now. They avoided personal topics at all costs. "If your brother had a motive, I don't know what it could be."

According to his men, Titos Demakis hadn't cared one way or another when news of the deaths arrived. "What a shame" were the only words he'd allowed in reaction, and apparently, they'd been as dry as toast.

"What about Apollon?" Oskar asked. If anyone on the council would act to protect their place, it would be him.

Emanouella's jaw tightened, and true, heated emotion flashed in her eyes. It was the first spark of life he'd seen in her since she returned.

"What?" he asked.

"Nothing." She jumped to her feet and stormed past him.

"Even if I didn't know you, I'd know that for the lie it is." Oskar maneuvered into her path and took her by the arm. "Is it possible he—"

Tears broke over her lower lids, and she shook her head. "He didn't do this. He wouldn't dare risk an element of his leverage over me."

Emanouella knew she'd made a mistake the moment she let the admission slip. She was no better than a dam weakened by time, barely holding back the truths she'd vowed to contain for the rest of her life. Grief had weakened her; she couldn't even *hear* Apollon's name without becoming visibly irate.

Oskar's tone dipped dangerously low. "What leverage?"

Breaking Oskar's heart all those years ago had been hard enough. She'd sworn against giving him a reason to fight the separation. Their relationship was never meant to last, anyway. That's what she told herself. She'd been lucky to have that time at all. Everyone should experience love and passion at least once in their life.

Reopening those wounds wasn't fair to him. Maybe it would make her feel better, but how would the truth benefit him? He didn't love her anymore, so what did it matter?

"Apollon knew what Angelos meant to me, that's all. He would sometimes threaten to tell Angelos about...things I'd done. Ruin my image in his eyes." She knuckled the last of her tears away. "I couldn't stomach the idea that my son thought less of me or believed

I was this imperfect human. He wasn't blind to my flaws, but there are parts of my past I'd rather he didn't know. Apollon knew that."

Oskar stepped back, his breath coming in small, frozen clouds. "Your past. You're talking about us."

Emanouella nodded and nearly started crying all over again. She couldn't stand seeing the hurt in his expression. "I never regretted a single moment. Please believe that."

"You never looked back, though, did you?"

Her eyelids fluttered wetly as she struggled to find the right response. "We both chose Perean. Our reasons might have differed, but you can't tell me you would have ever walked away from our people."

"I was never given the opportunity to make that choice."

Coming here had been a mistake. She still loved him—that had been undeniable these last few weeks—and his pain was hers. The idea that either of them could let the past go had been an absurd hope.

Emanouella stepped around him. "I have to go. Someone will have noted my absence."

"There was a time that didn't concern you," he called to her back.

Things were different now, but that was another thing she would rather he didn't question.

She paused, then swiveled ever-so-slightly to meet his gaze. "I'm sorry, Oskar. This was a mistake. You won't see me again."

<hr>

Oskar spent the first hour hating her. How dare she come back into his life as if nothing happened. As if none of it mattered. Had he *ever* mattered?

Eventually, the anger dissipated, and he heard what she *hadn't* said. Emanouella was hiding something, and he needed to find out what.

Over the next few days, he sent her messages the old way.

Without flowers, he sent bits of forest; dried leaves and slivers of grass. He didn't know how else to get her attention. And still, she never returned.

The one place he knew he could catch her was the temple. She visited often enough, especially since the deaths of her family. Even then, it was two weeks before she showed up.

As usual, she left her guards at the door and knelt before the statue of Ilenta. Those who had already knelt before the goddess caught sight of their queen and rose to pray elsewhere. Emanouella remained there for several minutes, silent tears streaming down her cheeks and dripping into her lap.

Oskar waited out of sight until she stood, relieved of her burdens. She angled to go, and he stepped into her eyeline. It had been many years since he last surprised her here, but she hadn't startled. Instead, she dipped her chin in the subtlest of nods and followed.

Several levels above the main temple, the priest's libraries were almost always quiet and dark. Oskar lit a taper in the windowless room that smelled of aged paper and must. Rows of books and scrolls packed the space for dozens of feet in either direction.

Emanouella arrived only minutes behind him, double-checking the corridor before closing them in. "If we're caught—"

"What exactly do you believe will happen? We're not doing anything. I'm the Master Blade of the Guild, investigating an assassination on your behalf. I can produce centuries of proof showing the number of times the royals have utilized our skills. Mihail Vidalatos, your husband's own brother, trusted us to—"

"Stop. Please stop." Emanouella lowered into the nearest chair and stared into the library shadows. "You know it's not that simple."

Oskar set aside the flickering taper and sat in a chair facing her. He so badly wished he had the right to unwind her hands. To feel the strength of those fingers and the softness of her palms. But he couldn't.

With a sigh, he lowered his chin. "I know it's not."

"I've spent the last two decades lying to myself." She met his eyes. "I almost let myself believe I never loved you. Not truly. Great affection at most. I had been so young at the time. How could I know what love truly felt like?"

Oskar slumped back in his chair. He'd never tried to discount what he'd felt. But their situations were quite different. He'd had no wife or family to answer to. "And now you know better?"

She nodded, and her throat bobbed deeply. "Nothing has changed for me. I still feel your absence like a painful weight on my chest. The need to touch you has only become stronger when you're near." Her hands came up and began emphasizing her words. "I'm ravenous for your mouth and breath on my skin—"

It took everything he had to remain still.

Emanouella reclined back and took a deep breath. "None of it changes things."

Oskar sat forward and braced on his knees. "The problem is, Em, I don't know what changed things in the first place."

"The gods. The prophecy. The fate of our lands. The lives my husband would snuff out for reasons I still don't fully understand."

"And Apollon? What's his exact role in all of this?"

"Apollon holds all of our strings."

* * *

Twenty-One Years Ago

Emanouella couldn't recall the last time she intentionally sought time with her husband, but she had to know if Oskar's assessment of him was correct. The coincidences surrounding Orestis, Apollon, and the assassinations of not only her eldest brother Tiberius, but Orestis's twin Mihail were too glaring. Then, add to that the mysterious disappearances of Nikos and Natalia, whose eyes matched the description of the lovers from the prophecy; none of it made sense.

86

Orestis knew something. Had possibly done something in the name of this prophecy. But what?

He would never tell her the truth, and it was too much of a risk to reveal what she knew. She could, however, pay close attention to any mention of Aura or Vasilis. Apollon himself had offered to wed the two young lovers with eyes of blue and brown, and Orestis spent more time in the temple than usual since learning Aura was an acolyte there.

So, Emanouella sat at Orestis's table and walked him to council meetings. She even warmed his bed at night, though he had no idea she wouldn't become with child—not with the tincture she dropped into her morning teas.

She also became quite adept at standing in his shadow, just out of sight. Listening.

Unfortunately, Apollon began to detect her proximity and was always careful with his words. Perhaps, too careful.

Emanouella had always thought of Apollon as Orestis's harmless companion. They were friends, for lack of a better word. But lately, she wondered if there was more to it. Orestis heeded Apollon's advice more than any other member of the council. Was it because he trusted the High Priest? Or was it something else?

When Orestis began questioning Emanouella's motives for their shared meals and long talks with her seemingly innocuous questions, she knew this was Apollon's influence. Just in time for her to overhear something vital.

"It's as I suspected," Apollon whispered to Orestis. They'd stepped outside into a veranda for privacy. "Their souls are tied to the fires within the mountain. It has to happen there, and to break the cycle, they must go in at the same time."

Orestis stared into the distance. "Let's not act hasty. We have them close at hand, and as long as they don't sense trouble, it won't be difficult to take them once we're ready."

"I've taken the girl into my confidence; she trusts me."

"And the boy?"

The boy? Vasilis?

"The boy has no plans of joining another merchant vessel anytime soon," Apollon replied. "Not until they've wed."

"Delay the ceremony as long as possible and leave no margin for error. We must ensure this happens exactly as it should."

"I might have a solution that gives us an additional measure of control. A cage inside the cavern with—"

The High Priest stiffened and began to swivel in Emanouella's direction.

Damn the gods. He'd sussed her out.

Emanouella rose from her seat where a garden hedge had mostly hidden her from view. Staring blindly at the book pages in her hand, she pretended to be so engrossed in the words that she hadn't noticed the men.

"How long have you been sitting there?" Orestis asked.

Emanouella feigned surprise, a hand to her heart. "I don't know. A long while, I think. Is everything all right?"

Apollon lifted a thick brow. "You mean to tell us you heard nothing we said?"

She returned his raised brow with one of her own. He might have some measure of power over the king, but he couldn't demand an answer from her, no matter how badly he wanted it.

However, there was one person who could, so she shifted her attention to Orestis and put forth the one thing that might sway him from doing so.

"Husband." Emanouella smiled prettily at Orestis. "I was going to write to my brother Titos this afternoon. Is there anything you would like me to pass on?"

The mention of the Sotteran king was the one thing that never failed to give Orestis pause. She never understood Titos's power over him and didn't care. Some sort of competition began before either of them was crowned. Orestis's response to her brother was a useful tool she deployed during desperate moments like this one. Almost as if the gentle reminder of her family's identity urged him to back off.

"No," Orestis said. "Nothing."

Emanouella bowed her head, then passed by at a casual pace. She didn't stop until she was well past the open doors into the palace. There, she hid behind the wall and waited.

"Your Majesty," Apollon said, "she heard—"

"She heard nothing she could make sense of. Even if she could, what exactly would she do with that information? Forget about her and have this cage fabricated. I want it installed inside the mountain as soon as possible."

* * *

Present Day

Oskar turned toward one of the library shelves, rubbing his jaw. He vividly remembered the day she warned him that Orestis and Apollon planned to make a move against the lovers and suggested he get them out of Perean. "That's how you knew what they planned."

Emanouella frowned at her lap and the hands she clasped there. "And that was the moment Apollon began to have me watched."

That, he hadn't known. "How closely?"

"Close enough to know about our affair. Thankfully, I never returned to your cottage after that. Your home remains a secret."

Emanouella stood and gathered her cloak around her. "He'll learn I was here. Can we talk more later? I'll come to you when I know it's safe."

His heart hurled against his ribcage. He'd put her in danger coming here. "What will you tell Apollon if he asks?"

"I don't know." She sighed. "The truth, I suppose. Or part of it, at least. I asked the Guild to investigate the assassinations."

Oskar could only nod, and neither of them moved to part ways. She held his gaze, and everything she'd admitted before lay there for the taking.

I still feel your absence like a painful weight on my chest.
I'm ravenous for your mouth and breath on my skin.

She still loved him, and gods help him, he would love her forever.

Emanouella stripped him of contact and turned for the door—

"Wait," he called, then ate up the space between them.

He reached for her, and she retreated only to mitigate the damage as his mouth claimed hers. She hit the wall with a *thunk*, and he started to pull away. "I'm sor—"

"Don't you dare stop." Emanouella gripped the back of his neck and arched her body into his just like she used to.

Oskar did stop, though, but only long enough to watch her gaze devour his mouth. The way she bit her lip. That was all he could handle, and with a squeeze of her hip, he took her mouth and tongue.

Within the darkness behind his lids, she was a deep, luxurious inhale and the rasping slide of her palms against his skin. Every creak of the floorboard was timed to her every shift in weight as she pushed her body closer and *closer*...

She was rose petals in fresh water and sweet spices in her morning tea. She was the cool brine skating off the bay at night.

And just like that, their cold history, the years they spent apart, broke in favor of sunlight and heat. For the love they'd held so tightly to for reasons beyond their imaginings.

Emanouella broke the kiss, though her body remained pressed warmly to his. She stroked his chin and ran a thumb over his bottom lip. "Go home," she whispered. "Wait for me."

"Is it safe?"

"I know what to do. Trust me."

Oskar paced the floor of his home and couldn't figure out what to do with his hands. One second, they were on his hips, the next at his sides, and the next, he pushed fingers through his hair. He sat, stood, paced, and started all over again.

If anything happened to her because of him—

Emanouella burst into the cabin wearing a gown similar to a palace maid's. It was constructed of cheap beige fabric with a thin, braided rope wrapped around her waist. Her cloak, too, was thin and dull gray.

"Were you seen?" he asked.

She shook her head and cleared her throat. "Oskar, I don't know what we're doing—"

"I love you." It was the only truth that mattered. That would *ever* matter.

Her fingers went to her lips, and silver lined her lower lids. "You do?"

He approached, hand outstretched. With all the barriers cast aside, he needed to touch her. The rest, they would figure out later.

Emanouella stepped into his arms. She traced the scar through his left eyebrow, then the one across his jaw. "I hate that he did this to you."

He kissed the space between her brows. "None of my scars changed who I am or what you mean to me."

She brought his mouth to hers. The kiss skimmed like a whisper, all tentative breath and gentle brushes. Her lips parted in time with his, and he stroked her tongue, tasting her.

That was all it took. Oskar erupted into her and pushed her toward the bed.

8

Emanouella bloomed beneath Oskar's body. Spread her petals for his sunlight. Drank of his nectar.

His weight, his scent, his touch was more than she'd allowed to resurface in her memory over their lost decades. When she touched herself at night, it was to faded, trivial memories. The real thing was a powerful aphrodisiac. Her body was erupting with violent heat and sparking nerves.

Oskar's tongue filled her mouth as his hands groped toward her hips, fingers clawing deep groves into her skin. His hard length pressed against her, teasing and promising.

"I need you," she said once she managed to breathe. The ache between her legs was unbearable. "I need you inside me."

He moaned, and his jaw muscles flared. "I'm never letting you get away again."

She smiled. "I'm yours. Even absent, I've always been yours."

Emanouella didn't know how they'd get through this, but she refused to believe her life was only this. Queen to a malevolent king and mother to a spiteful daughter. Didn't she deserve this man's love? A life away from all that?

She yanked his tunic up and, together, they tossed the fabric to the floor. Then she was rolling, their legs scissored, until she was on top. Together, they untied her belt and removed her dress. The cool air made her skin erupt in gooseflesh, and her nipples peaked.

Oskar sat up and filled his mouth with her breast. She clawed his hair and held him close, her insides a liquid heat.

Then their mouths collided, tongues sliding, and his erection demanded release from within his pants. She rocked her hips deep into his lap.

He grunted and hurriedly worked his pants open and down.

Emanouella fisted his erection, finding it hot and soft and solid. She guided his shaft toward her center and paused. Met his eyes. Basked in everything they'd once been and still were despite their long absence. Love, friendship, passion, trust. The promise of his body and soul.

She stroked his cheek. "I love you." Then she sank onto his erection.

His eyes widened, and he took her in a deep, luxurious kiss.

Her inner walls sparked like lightning, and she groaned. She took him as deep as she could, then waited for her body to adjust.

Oskar's fingers clawed up her back, and he set his forehead against her breastbone. "Gods, woman. I forgot how good you feel."

He rolled her beneath him and pulled out to the tip, leaving her empty and wanting and near begging. Then he filled her again. And again. And again.

Emanouella thawed. The restraints of her world fell away, and she was reminded of what it was like to love someone so deeply that she would destroy the world. She would take every risk for him. Take every pain meant for his body. Accept a life devoid of warmth if it meant he could live.

Even now, she would do it all, all over again.

———

I t was hard to focus, and Oskar desperately wanted to stay in this moment with her. He needed to remember every second of this time in a way he hadn't before.

Years ago, they'd fucked, and they'd made love. They ravaged each other outdoors and in. On beds and against walls. They'd tasted each other's bodies from top to bottom. He'd been able to read her body as easily as words on a page.

And now, she was beginning the climb to orgasm. He knew she would come because of how she bit her lip and that glassy look in her eyes. The way she drove her hips up toward his, synching their movements. She was never more beautiful to him than when flushed like this. Raw. Trusting with her body.

Oskar maneuvered her arms up past her head and clasped her wrists together. Her back arched toward him, and her head burrowed into the pillow, opening her neck for his mouth and tongue.

Then they were kissing again, frantic. Their hands roamed all over their naked skin. She gripped his shoulders and dug into his back. He stroked her thighs to her knees, hooking her legs around his hips. All of this was familiar, yet new. Their bodies had seen more years, but the response was the same.

A whimper escaped Emanouella—she was close. She was so wet, and so tight, and he begged his own orgasm off—he wouldn't go without her.

She panted and clawed and moaned.

Oskar moved faster, deeper, harder—

Emanouella's body seized beneath him. Her inner walls pulsed around his cock, and she released a cry full of release and abandon.

He gave into the pressure of his orgasm, and only then did he allow his mind the freedom to disassociate. His entire body was a flash of heat and pleasure and pulsing release, and he'd never felt closer to this woman than he did in those few seconds.

The feeling was gone as soon as it began, and they were Oskar and Emanouella again. Assassin and Queen. Protector and Regent.

Two people at their most vulnerable, and he'd just taken her like a starving man. Attacked her body with utter abandon.

She was the one woman in their realm with which he should take the utmost care and never could.

Emanouella smiled, and a light entered her tawny eyes.

An incredible lightness filled his chest, and he stroked her hair back. "How much time do we have?"

"Hours."

"Good. I plan to make all of them count."

T he entire world slumbered but for them. When they weren't frantically devouring each other, they made love. Sleep threatened to take them a few times, but they refused to give in. Not when their time was so limited.

Their needs eventually slowed, and Oskar heated water for a shared bath. They naturally fell into position, just like they used to: her between his legs, back to his chest. Her head hung back on his shoulder, and he traced wet fingers in and out of the water, up and down her arm.

"We have to talk about what happened," he finally said. Hated to say. The last thing he wanted was to break this bubble of bliss. However, they couldn't continue acting as if nothing happened. And he still didn't know the full extent of Apollon's part in all of this.

Emanouella sighed. "I know."

"Last I saw you, everything was fine. Hristos and I went to get Aura and Vasilis—"

"And you were captured."

He nodded, then kissed her temple. "I didn't see you after that."

Twenty-One Years Ago

Emanouella would prefer physical torture to this.

Apollon, a man who had somehow ascended to his wealth and power through a prophecy and a king, now mirrored her from the settee in her own apartments, his presence a looming threat.

And then there was the regiment of armed guards blockading her exits.

"On the king's orders," Apollon had said when he'd arrived, his voice dripping with an unsettling mix of authority and ambiguity. "For your protection."

Then he sat. And she sat.

And that was how they remained for several minutes.

She suspected he wanted her to speak first. To ask questions. He needed her to divulge information and somehow insinuate herself in the crimes he hoped to accuse her of.

Emanouella nearly sighed in relief when Apollon moved first. He shifted and pulled a small, familiar bottle from his robes. He shook the contents, watching the clear liquid and tiny bits of dried herbs slosh.

Her throat closed, and her entire body went still. It was the tincture she put in her daily tea to prevent pregnancy. How had he gotten it? Did he or someone else go through her things?

Pain shot through her jaw as she clenched. "What are you doing with that?"

"What has me curious, Your Majesty, is if you take this because you didn't want to give your husband another child, or because you needed to hide the affair? Or both?"

This time, she couldn't hide her surprise as her jaw fell open of its own accord. "Affair? How dare you—"

"You're going to pretend there's no one? You were seen together. Alone. In my own temple, no less."

Her mouth went dry. She and Oskar had met the other day in one of the private prayer rooms, but nothing had happened. She told Oskar about what she overheard, and they discussed helping the lovers escape Perean. Apparently, that was all the motivation Apollon needed to search her rooms. They'd been so careful otherwise.

"Clever of you," he continued, "to choose a Blade to consort with. Anger them, and they could decide to assassinate the king."

"They're not like that."

"No?"

Her voice dipped low. "No. And I didn't 'choose' anything. Not that I owe you an explanation. We love each other."

Apollon barked a laugh. "Whatever you say, Your Majesty."

"Does my husband know?"

"I keep nothing from him. You should know that by now." He shifted, reclining deeper into his authority. "You really shouldn't have told your lover what you heard. I hear he's not doing very well."

Emanouella straightened, and a scorching heat broke out across her palms and forehead. "What do you mean? What are you saying?"

Apollon smirked. "You didn't know we had him? I'm surprised. The king is with him now."

For a time, Oskar could combat the pain and savagery by slipping into recent memories. Her smile, her laugh, her scent. The ease with which she gave over to him, body and soul.

But even he had his breaking point, and with his arms hung, suspended from the ceiling, he had no choice but to take the relentless beatings. One strike in particular opened the skin over his eye. The unnamed soldiers had stripped him of his clothes long ago, and his brand gave him away. This only intrigued them more. What did a Blade want with two commoners?

No one knew why he and Hristos went to Vasilis and Aura's home or why they had booked passage for the lovers, who hadn't known themselves. The Blades thought they had the advantage by arriving under the cover of night, and the couple was caught completely off-guard.

They hadn't planned for how Orestis and Apollon had put soldiers in place to watch the lovers. They'd immediately moved in to capture all four of them. Now, Oskar was alone in this cold, damp cell. Hristos was likely in a similar situation.

The lovers...? He didn't know. Would the king torture them before taking them to the cage they'd prepared in the mountain? The only thing he could gather was that Orestis needed them alive when they were dropped into the fires. That was the only way to ensure a true death of their bonded souls.

Sleep was Oskar's only reprieve from the lost sensation in his shoulders. Based on his level of hunger and thirst, he'd been there a while. A full day. Maybe two. Three? It wasn't clear.

When the beatings didn't produce answers, Orestis appeared, crownless and plainly outfitted in a chiton and sandals. They were the same age, though the king didn't look quite as hardened.

The king dismissed everyone from the room and reclined against the wall. "You're the one from the arena. You jumped into it to save your queen."

There was no reason to deny it, so Oskar gave a single nod.

"According to my wife, you drowned, and she was rescued—half-dead—by some fisherman. Nursed back to health on a ship docked outside the bay by people who didn't speak our language." Orestis pushed off the wall and strode closer. "My wife, I'm beginning to learn, is a very good liar."

Oskar refused to take the bait and clenched his jaw.

"She told you about my plans, didn't she?" The king scrubbed his jaw. "And if I hadn't listened to Apollon's council and put men there to watch them, you would have helped the lovers disappear."

Oskar lifted his chin and met his gaze, unblinking. The only answer he'd give.

Orestis swung with an impressive backhand, his ring slicing Oskar's cheek open. Tendrils of thick blond waves fell across the king's forehead. "Do you think you're *helping* these people? They're plotting treason against the crown."

"Is that what you said about Nikos and Natalia?"

This took the king onto his back foot. "I haven't heard those names in some time, but now I understand. You knew the male because he was in your Order."

"I did."

"So this is some kind of revenge for his death?"

The words landed like a hammer that knocked the wind out of him. Assuming Nikos was dead and knowing were very different.

The king smirked. "Shall I tell you how they died?" He put his mouth near Oskar's ear. "We dragged the male into the executioner's courtyard and laid him out on the guillotine. I wanted the female to watch, so we held her nearby. She screamed and screamed and *screamed*..." He pulled back to meet Oskar's eyes. "She practically climbed onto the table after that. Might have pulled the handle herself if it were possible. Isn't that strange? She *wanted* to die.

"Anyway," he continued, stepping away. "I had them both quietly executed right under my father's nose. He was too busy dealing with my brother's assassination at the time, and it all went unrecorded."

Oskar's stomach turned. "Why?" The question ground out as if dragged across coarse sand.

"The two souls, with eyes of earth and sky, will set upon a journey to return the lost heir to the land of sea and steel."

"The prophecy?"

"Don't pretend as if I'm the only one in this room who believes it to be true. Nikos and Natalia have returned as Vasilis and Aura, and you were going to put them on a ship to fulfill their role in locating the missing heir."

Oskar didn't know what to say to any of that. He must have gone over that prophecy a million times. Some of it he was able to comprehend.

Emanouella's betrothal to Orestis, for example, was the marriage of enemies.

The mention of eyes like earth and sky was easy to attribute to Nikos and Natalia, and now Vasilis and Aura. He knew of no one else with eyes like theirs.

The land of sea and steel was Perean.

To this day, he didn't fully understand much of it. Honestly, it didn't matter. He didn't care what Orestis or even the gods' motivations were—young, innocent people shouldn't have to suffer for this man's gain. If there was a missing heir—he didn't see how there could be—that was the king's problem, not his.

"My part in this isn't as grand as you seem to think," Oskar said.

"It doesn't matter. I have the lovers, and unlike the other two, I know how to stop their souls from returning."

"You've gone mad. They've done nothing to you, nor do they have plans outside of living their lives together."

Orestis shook his head. "Other than my wife, who else knows?"

Oskar clamped his jaw shut.

The king swung open the door. He motioned to someone, and several guards appeared and threw Hristos inside. The old man was in a similar state to Oskar. Beaten, bloody, face barely recognizable, and naked.

The king fisted a handful of hair on Hristos's crown and forced the two Blades to look at each other. "Where's the heir?"

Hristos sneered and spit blood across the concrete.

The king looked Oskar in the eyes. "Tell me everything, or he dies."

Oskar didn't know where to focus his attention: Hristos with fury blazing in his eyes or the king who had gone completely mad. "We know nothing about an heir."

"You'll have to kill me," Hristos ground out. "Because I can promise you this: we may not know anything about an heir now, but after tonight, the Guild will make it their mission to find out."

Flames erupted in the king's eyes as he held Oskar's full attention. "Once I kill him, I'll have no choice but to bring her in and offer you her life in his place. Will you watch Emanouella die the way Natalia did Nikos? Will you scream for her as she dies?"

His heartbeat became a hammer strike. "You wouldn't."

"Wouldn't I?"

With his teeth grit, Orestis plunged a blade through Hristos's eye.

Oskar roared.

⸻

Present Day

Oskar shivered behind Emanouella in the cooling bath. He stroked the top of her head with a damp hand and nuzzled his nose into her temple. "He never kept that promise," he said. "To this day, I still don't know why he didn't kill me as well."

Emanouella turned sideways to meet his eyes. "It was a part of the deal I made with Apollon. I'm not sure why Orestis agreed to it— maybe he was just that desperate for another child."

Oskar straightened. "You bargained for my life by promising him another child? Em, why?"

"Because there is nothing—*nothing*, Oskar—that I wouldn't do for you. Nothing." A line of tears formed along her lower lids and wet her long lashes. "The bargain was all very complicated, but it all came down to my connection to Soterra. One word from me and my brother would keep them out of the mountain, and..." Her throat bobbed. "If anything happens to you or me, a missive will be hand-delivered directly to my brother. Orestis's secrets will be no more.

"I had to tell them everything we knew," she continued, her chin lowering, "which wasn't much. Not enough to concern them, at any rate. I wasn't to interfere with their plans, which I managed to do anyway. Not that they could prove it."

"The soldier's uniform," he said, understanding. "Did you bring that yourself?"

She laughed, though it was dark and without humor. "No. I sent my handmaid Chrysanthi with the uniform and the note. I instructed her to leave them for you and that you would know what to do. I also arranged for her passage out of Perean, just in case, and Apollon assumed she'd acted alone."

Oskar stroked her cheek. "You took a huge risk."

"There's more."

Disbelief and awe tore through him. How much more could she have done?

"I got to the boy first. Orestis and Apollon never knew he'd even been born."

Oskar surged forward, sloshing the water. "What? Where is he? *Who* is he?"

She shook her head. "I'll take that answer to my grave. It's safer that way."

The Guild lived by a similar code. The name of a target was never spoken aloud unless their guilt was guaranteed and their death imminent. If Oskar were to be captured again, there was no telling what Orestis would do for that vital information. Without it, Selene was never safer.

"I was too late to hide Selene," Emanouella said. "The best I could do was keep her close. I don't know what Orestis had planned to do with her at the time, but he was going to kill Ioanna, and I couldn't allow it. Taking them as slaves was the only thing I could think to do."

Oskar had known they'd taken Selene as a slave, and he'd devised ways to see her or her mother often these last nineteen years, befriending them both. He'd even taken to using Selene for information every now and then. Mostly, he liked seeing the spark of life in her eyes when assigned a task.

"I'm glad you did," he said. "She seems well enough and safe—

which is all that matters. I wish I could get her and her mother out safely."

He'd offered to help Selene escape many times, but she refused to leave without Ioanna. They'd have to move quickly, and the king wouldn't let Selene go so easily. He'd never stop hunting her. A trip such as this, rife with dangers and the need to flee at a moment's notice, would be difficult for Ioanna, who walked with a severe limp after a bad femur break didn't heal right.

A part of him was wary, too, after the last attempt to save the lovers went awry.

Oskar kissed Emanouella and stroked her hair. "It's over now. We can figure out a way to move on."

She nodded. "I'd like that. Maybe we can have that future we used to dream about."

"No maybes. Not this time. We're getting out of here. As soon as we figure out who's responsible for killing your son."

9

For years, Emanouella marked time just like everyone else: by hours, days, weeks, and months. By events such as weddings and births. By the arrival of visitors. There was even a time when she depended heavily on the appearance of her courses.

Then Angelos and the children died, and time existed in revolutions of bad and worse. Heartache and devastation. She'd never felt more seen without being recognized.

Hours then entered the whirl of time where her entire world belonged to someone else. She wasn't the mother who knelt in her son's blood, holding his head. She was the woman Oskar cherished. That, more than anything else, solidified her decision.

She'd given more than enough to the life her father gave as a bargaining chip.

"Does it bother you that we lost so much time?" she asked Oskar one evening. They'd just made love atop the furs before a blazing fire and lay with tangled limbs and gratified breaths. "All of our good years are behind us."

His chest jumped on a quiet laugh. "You're all of two and forty, and you have plenty of good years ahead. Take it from me; I've already lived some of them, and I like to think I've got quite a few more left."

Emanouella rose to an elbow and peered down at him. "What if we could have more?"

Oskar didn't hesitate for a moment after hearing the idea that followed. In fact, he threw himself into the details that took weeks to solidify. He, like her, found her idea fitting when so much of their time together had involved the prophecy and reincarnation of lovers. And now, her snooping through Apollon's notes on the matter wouldn't go to waste.

However, the priest's records hadn't prepared her for the uncomfortable heat within the Ethereal Mountain. Sharp rocks, like frozen teeth, dripped from the ceiling and rose from the floor. They could have been standing within the gaping maw of a real-life dragon, its fire bubbling and ready to erupt on a single exhale.

Oskar's attention drifted past all those details and halted on the cage her husband and Apollon had installed. The very place where Aura and Vasilis had died.

She shivered as if the ghosts of their poor souls passed through her. That was impossible, she knew. Even so, knowing how they'd died...

Emanouella squeezed Oskar's hand. "Come. I think it's over here."

They climbed the stone dais and stood over the broken marble shaped like an octagon with gold veins running through it.

Oskar lifted her chin. "Are you ready?"

Most days, it was hard to read the look in his eyes. It was a part of what made him good at his profession. Now, though, Emanouella read it all. His love for her, the trust in all those ancient markings, the faith—no, the *hope*—that this would work.

She set her hand in his. "I'm ready."

Emanouella marked time much differently after that day. She had only forever and ever and ever with smaller moments of her old reality filtered in. Reminders that she wasn't quite away from it all.

There were many loose ends to tie up. An assassin still walked free, and Selene was still marked for death. Emanouella was still the queen consort, and Oskar was still the leader of the Blades.

Some weeks, Emanouella considered whether she truly needed the name of Angelos's murderer. There were often days she thought Selene's destiny was exactly where it belonged: in the hands of the gods. Who were they to think themselves powerful enough to help her?

This was the grief talking. She was so desperate to start her forever with Oskar, to be in rooms that didn't hold so many ghosts, that she would give it all up and never look back. She needed a life that no one had orchestrated for the benefit of everyone else.

Oskar, however, remained focused. "Tell me about Alexandra."

They were on one of their walks through the forest, and today was special. The last frost had long melted away, and the days were growing warmer. Spring scented the air. Worms tilled the earth, and bees pollinated the flowers. Birds built their nests high in the treetops.

Any day now, the wildflowers would bloom.

A fitting time, she thought with a flutter in her belly.

"Em?" Oskar squeezed her hand, forcing her back to his question.

She frowned. "Alexandra is a lot like her father." It shamed her to speak so honestly of her own daughter, but of anyone in the world, she could speak her truth to Oskar. "I have to be careful around her at times. She can react quite negatively when things don't go her way."

"How did she take it when she was named the king's heir?"

Her memory of that time felt like wading through thick mud. "I don't recall that time well. She's accepted it and appears to have taken it with ease. Why do you ask?"

His smile flashed tightly, and he pulled her close to his side. "Just curious."

They stepped out of the woods and into a sea of tall grass and flowers that had yet to open.

Oskar's smile reached his eyes as he took it all in. "It looked just like this that year I came back. I wouldn't be surprised if we find a rare bloom within." His expression faltered, and his smile dipped towards a frown. "A blue one, perhaps."

Like the flower he left her during that visit to the temple. She'd lived entire lifetimes since then. They both had.

Emanouella took his hand. "Where did you just go?"

Oskar scanned the field, squinting through the sunlight. "Every year, these flowers bloom, and it feels like they'll live forever. But they always die. Everything fades."

"Oh, my love," she whispered, taking his face in both hands. "Not all blooms fade in the end. Our love didn't."

His chin dipped. "It did once. It could again."

She shook her head. "Oskar, no," she began, voice quivering. "It won't."

"You can't know that."

"We won't let it. I'm—" She swallowed the lump in her throat and released the smile she'd held back since arriving. "We're having a baby."

<hr>

Oskar thought he knew fear. He'd been standing at the bottom of an hourglass with sand trickling from above, the threat of Emanouella's life on the outside. A knife over her head. But he'd had time. He could—and would—keep her safe.

Now, those grains of sand were coming down in a furious rain, and they were on fire.

He was losing time too fast.

He was closer to naming the assassin and, if he was right—

Gods. He needed this to be wrong.

And Selene… She was only a couple of weeks from turning twenty. How could he leave her alone when she likely had only a year? At this point, he was considering ways to get her and her mother out and taking the risk of Ioanna's limp slowing down their escape. There had to be a way to make this work.

"I'm booking you passage on a ship to Okos," he told Emanouella the week following her announcement. "I'll stay behind and finish things up here."

He had to get her out of harm's way so he could focus on the rest.

Emanouella glittered like the queen she was, knelt before Ilenta's statue, head hung in prayer, while he stood only feet away in the shadow of a column.

Her shoulders tensed. "What? No, Oskar—"

"I have a contact there who will forge your new identity and put you on another ship—"

"No," she hissed a little too loudly. People nearby looked over with expressions of curiosity and annoyance. Emanouella shifted on her knees and waited for their attention to fade. "We'll leave together."

"I can't finish up here and worry about you at the same time. Think of our child."

Her next breath quivered. "I'm beginning to think we're taking too big a risk. Maybe we should just go."

Oskar had considered this very idea more times than he could count, especially since learning about the baby. But he'd spent damn near forty years mixed up in this mess with the lovers and the prophecy.

Nikos and Natalia had been his family, and maybe he hadn't known Vasilis and Aura well, but he'd looked into the male's eyes and saw Nikos in there. Oskar risked his life to ensure they could live again.

As for Selene, he loved this girl like a daughter. An unexpected development, to be sure, but no less true. She didn't deserve the life she'd been dumped into, and there was little he could do about it at the moment. Her escape had to be handled with the utmost care—and only when she was willing—or she'd be hunted for the rest of her days.

And he had to ensure Selene was in the opposite direction of Emanouella. He'd never forgive himself if Emanouella were caught in the crossfire to get Selene.

But they couldn't have this conversation here without notice from Apollon or his people.

It was days before Emanouella could get away again, and he was startled to see her looking so gray from sickness. She moved as if the world spun counter to her direction.

"You can't get away with this for long," he said, helping her into a chair before his cold fireplace. "You must leave."

Emanouella sank slowly into her seat and closed her eyes. "I know. People are beginning to ask questions."

He knelt before her and set a hand on her knee. "My men are ready to stage your death on my command. It's all planned."

Her beautiful, tawny eyes drifted open. "You'll come with me?"

His heart sank. "You know I can't. Not until I can ensure Selene's safety."

"The same way you've located my son's murderer?"

Oskar flinched at the accusation in her tone. He'd made her a promise, and yes, it sounded like he would be willing to set that aside. She didn't yet know that he already had her answer, and it wasn't one he could ever prepare her for.

"I'm sorry," she said and blew out a breath. "That wasn't fair. I know you've tried."

Oskar rose and paced away. "Did you know there are passages beneath the palace? Rooms?"

"No. What are you talking about?"

He quickly explained how he'd located the original plans for the palace in the Guild's archives and how Blades have used these tunnels to get in and out throughout the years.

"One of the tunnels," he finished, "connects directly to the royal nursery."

She was sitting forward now, gripping the arms of her chair. "You're saying he came in through there—" Her gaze turned distant. "He took my grandsons because they saw too much, didn't he? If they'd been somewhere else—"

"No, Em. The assassin was clearing the line of succession."

Emanouella's head shook, slow and even. "Succession?"

Oskar felt sick. "The time between when the boys were last seen and when they were...delivered—" He paused to let her adjust to his words. "They weren't taken from the palace grounds, and we believe Angelos was lured in by the threat to his children. My men found the room inside the tunnels and the weapon used."

White hot rage shot through her eyes, and she stood. "Who's weapon was it?"

"A handmaid of Alexandra's, a girl named Meropi, identified it."

"I know who she is. What did she say?" Emanouella was breathing too fast, and he stepped forward to urge her to sit. "Don't touch me," she shouted. "Who killed my family, Oskar?"

"It was your daughter. Alexandra killed them."

The world was too loud. Her heartbeat too close to her ears. Emanouella's feet scraped the floor like blades sharpened across a whetstone. The front door creaked like a tree felled by an axe, and banshees screamed bloody murder into the wind outside.

In some distant place, she climbed her horse, and Oskar called her name. His touch scalded, but she was a hostage of the world and its living, pulverizing breath. None of this, yet *all* of this, was happening to her.

She had to go home.

She couldn't stay.

There was too much *air* here.

Too much truth.

Too much hope.

Her head too full of memories that shouldn't cause pain, yet she bled hot tears for miles over every single one.

Angelos had held baby Alexandra so sweetly, so lovingly, so innocently. *"I will protect her from the whole world, Momma."*

But who protected him from her?

He'd loved her so much and wanted to give her everything. He considered her and her well-being every single day of his life.

Inside the stables, the ghosts of two young boys raced toward her, laughing and red-faced. The very image of their father. *"Grandma-ma! Auntie Alexandra is chasing us! She says she'll get us!"*

Emanouella turned outside the stall and vomited into the dirt.

Men rushed toward her—stable hands?—wondering who she was and what she thought she was doing. Then they saw her face and bowed and groveled, and she didn't care.

She stumbled toward the palace and the ghosts and the cold, echoing halls. The all-seeing eyes and loose tongues.

People stopped to watch her around every turn, up every stair. Very few dared to ask, "My Lady, are you well?"

Emanouella had no throat to speak from. No tongue inside her mouth to aid her in a response.

She reached the top of the stairs and looked down the corridor that would take her toward the royal wing. Her heartbeat was back in her ears, and her breath chafed.

"Mother?"

Emanouella's body turned toward the sound, her conscious mind a beat behind.

Alexandra glowed with the ease of a star. Flawless in her beauty. Hair up in her usual twists and curls—Selene's work. She wore a chiton in a pale shade of green with gold accents.

"Mother?" she repeated, brown eyes scraping up and down

Emanouella's length. "What are you wearing? Have you been *outside* looking like that?"

The world came roaring back, full and heavy and electric. No one had known she'd left, but they would now. How many people watched their queen walk by in the dress of a scullery maid? Apollon would know within the hour, and Orestis—

Inside her mind, Emanouella let loose a scream that would make everyone bleed. She imagined clawing at her hair and dropping to her knees with such abandon that her kneecaps broke. She would bring this entire palace down on everyone if she had any true power at all.

"You are the daughter of a king, Emanouella." Her mother's spirit stood regally beside her, staring down the gentle slope of her nose. *"Let no one see what's really inside. Now, smile. That will always be your greatest weapon."*

Emanouella spread her lips until her teeth showed, and the area beside her eyes wrinkled. "Hello, my darling." She fingered her cheap gown. "This? This is a long, boring story."

Alexandra came forward and took her hand. "You've been crying." She frowned—she always had the most adorable pout, didn't she? "Have you been thinking about Angelos and the boys again?"

Heat flashed through her, but she remained perfectly still and held her expression. "The grief hits me at the worst times, it seems. I'll be all right."

The corridor filled suddenly with the approaching, regimented steps of the Royal Guard. Orestis appeared around the corner first, followed by four of his men. His glance was cursory at first, then pointed.

Emanouella had never been caught outside her silks in front of her family, and she felt naked under his scrutiny.

"You hold your own power," her mother said. *"You will one day be a queen. Own it."*

Her shoulders went back, and she performed her own scan of her husband and then her daughter. Murderers, both of them. Without a thought for the innocent lives they surrounded themselves with. Millions of people depended on their ability to rule and protect, and their primary concern was holding onto that godsdamned throne.

They didn't deserve any of it.

Emanouella heard Oskar's voice now, from decades ago. The two of them were sitting atop their bluff, overlooking the capital. *"If you could do anything in the world, what would you do?"*

She loved Perean. She cared about its people. She'd given all of herself to ensure they had a hopeful future with Angelos as their king, and now that hope was gone.

"That's easy. I would be the sort of queen that would have made my parents proud."

As queen, there was only so much she could do, but her mother had taught her well. Had given her the tools to play the game and play it well. Orestis and Alexandra might be winning now, but she wasn't without a weapon in this fight.

"What is going on here?" Orestis asked.

"Nothing, husband." Emanouella shared her smile with him. "I need to change. Have you had dinner? We should sit down to eat together."

Alexandra's eyebrows drew together as her gaze flicked between her parents.

Orestis, too, seemed perplexed. He looked upon her as if she wore a second head. "I'll arrange a private dinner for us in my chambers."

"Good. I will see you later, then, my love."

Emanouella turned from her murderous family and set a hand over her belly.

Her final hope.

And the means to their utter destruction.

IO

"Northeast tower." Elias swallowed, his throat bobbing low. *"The true king lives, Oskar. Mihail li—"*

Oskar hurled awake in bed and gasped for air. His heart raced and stuttered as his head filled with memories that hadn't crossed his mind in decades.

Nikos squeezing Oskar's shoulder and smiling. *"Prince Mihail is a good man, and he'll be an even better king. Things won't always be like this."*

The last time he saw Nikos, he hurried onto a horse. *"I must go. The prince needs me."* Then, just before he kicked the horse into a full run, he said, *"Watch out for Natalia until I return."*

That turned into a promise Oskar was never able to keep.

Elias left Oskar with his dying message days ago, and his hands had never felt more tied.

Emanouella had gone silent and ignored all of his usual messages. He'd known she wouldn't take the truth well, but he hadn't foreseen this reaction. Did she blame him? Was that it? The way she'd left him that night...

As if she no longer inhabited her own body.

As if his words couldn't be heard.

He'd never seen her like that before, and if he couldn't reach her, could anyone?

She was alive—he knew that much, at least—and nothing abnormal was happening within the palace. According to his sources, the queen spent her days as she always did: entertaining courtiers, corresponding with the regions of Perean in the most need, and grieving in silence.

Her absence was like suffocating in slow motion. The days were cold despite the heat, and there was never enough food or water to give his body what he required to survive.

Oskar needed the reassurance that they were okay, but he also needed her help. If Mihail Vidalatos truly lived, this changed *everything*.

Of his few remaining contacts, no one had access to the northeast tower. Nor did they know anything about its occupant. Or that anyone, save for the shadows, lived inside it at all.

The one person he could think of with that sort of freedom was Emanouella.

Where was she?

This thought gnawed at him throughout the day, and he was no closer to an answer when her ghost appeared in the market.

No, not a ghost. Alexandra. She could be her mother's twin. It was eerie how much she resembled Emanouella.

Selene trailed the princess, tension a living thing in her expression and across her shoulders. She'd grown into a beautiful young woman and smart enough to outlive many others like her who were born into slavery. Oskar often wished he could bring her into the Guild and train her. She had this innate ability to become invisible and detect important details.

Alexandra took advantage of this quite a bit, actually. Oskar, too. He'd learned a lot through Selene's sleuthing, and the girl could access every level of the palace with a key Alexandra herself had provided.

Oskar watched the princess from the shadows of an alley, arms folded. She paused over tables and smiled at merchants. Disgust roiled in his gut. What sort of person could swing a sword through the necks of children, then turn around and convince the rest of the world that they were kind and good? Not even the king could manage that level of foolery.

Selene chewed her lip, fingers nervously playing with the belted chain around her waist.

Something was wrong.

He soon realized what had her so tense. Where were the Royal Guard? Leaving the palace without protection? That was a stupid thing to do.

Alexandra said something that made Selene freeze. Then the princess spat at her, "Why are you dawdling? Go."

Selene spun and fled down the street.

The gods just handed Oskar the opening he needed.

PART THREE

A SEA OF ECHOES

II

Emanouella despised the ruse. The false smiles. The soft touches. The whispering sighs and distant looks of a mother climbing and clawing from her grief. All the parts she had to play to disrupt Orestis and Alexandra's plans. To avoid unwanted attention.

The worst part was over, at least. She'd lain with Orestis.

Nothing about his methods had changed. Not the cold way he disrobed her and laid her across his bed. Not his soulless and hollow touch. There was no joy or passion.

No devotion.

No love.

The quickness with which he'd finished had been a small blessing, and she'd cried for days afterward, guilt-ridden and disgusted.

Oskar would never forgive her.

But she would do anything for Angelos, Dimos, and Faidon. For Selene and Augustus, who was now a grown man out in the vast world.

Most of all, she would do whatever it took for the Perean people.

Emanouella waited to reveal her pregnancy until the last

possible moment. She'd grown too sick to avoid seeing a healer, and people were growing suspicious. Word would soon spread. It was time Orestis learned he would soon be a father again.

She almost couldn't stomach the dinner she forced on them all. Alexandra wouldn't *stop talking*, constantly seeking Emanouella's attention. After weeks of playing the part of Alexandra's doting mother, she couldn't rise to it tonight. Maybe it was because of the constant sickness.

Or maybe it was because Orestis's gaze across the table was akin to a cold spear he hurled over and over and over.

Did he already know? Did it matter? What could he say? What would he do? He certainly couldn't disprove her claim that he had fathered the child.

Dinner plates were beginning to clear, and time was running out. Orestis and Alexandra discussed her betrothal, and Emanouella couldn't sit through yet another argument.

She cleared her throat and pasted on that smile she couldn't feel. "I have wonderful news."

Orestis's eyes all but said, *Finally, you will get to the point of this dinner.* But his only response was, "Oh?"

"I am with child."

Alexandras's fork hit her plate, but Emanouella held her husband's gaze and hoped her thoughts translated to him like the weapon she intended them to be. She would raise this child with the Vidalatos name and put him or her on his precious throne. Her child, made from the deepest form of love Emanouella had ever known, whose blood was that of someone good and kind, would rule Perean, and no one would be the wiser.

Emanouella went into the evening prepared for many reactions, but she hadn't stopped to consider her own. She would regret it for the rest of her life. Her feelings got the better of her, and maybe Alexandra had beat too long and too hard on her walls.

Maybe Orestis was still capable of hurting her feelings. "Is it even mine?"

She'd never hated him more.

And then Alexandra, finally dropping her own facade. "Hoping for a boy, I assume."

Emanouella couldn't take it anymore and spoke her mind for the first time in weeks. "You are my greatest shame."

And because of her loose tongue, Selene paid a near-deadly price the moment Emanouella turned her back.

The following day, a man of her Queen's Guard handed her an envelope. One of dozens she'd received over the weeks, but this would be different. This one would hold accusations and anger without saying a word.

With tears tracking down her cheeks, Emanouella set a corner of the sealed missive over a flame and let it burn to ash.

To Shadi Silver Wolf, Matriarch of Yiria
From Emanouella Vidalatos, Her Majesty the Queen
of Perean

Dearest Shadi,

I write to you with fondness and hope you receive this well.

Many years ago, you held my hand during one of my greatest moments of sadness. I have regretted never having thanked you and your triad in person for your kindness. While the moment between us was brief, your impact was great. My respect for you and your strength, your convictions, has only grown as I have witnessed how you care for your people.

It is for my people and yours that I write to you now. I offer you the truth as I know it, to do with what you will.

My son, the crown prince Angelos, and his heirs have been murdered by my own daughter, the princess Alexandra. Orestis has named her his heir, and I can't in good conscience allow her this level of power and authority. My people deserve better.

Orestis, too, has become consumed by a prophecy threatening his Seat. I do not yet know the extent of his crimes, but I can imagine they are just as great. No one, regardless of past or future alliances, is safe.

Even greater than that, I believe something is coming for us all. I fear I'm fighting a losing battle against the will of the gods themselves, and my husband is playing right into their hands. I am doing what I can to stop him, but I am alone. I fear for my people and the child I now carry, who holds my every remaining hope in his or her unborn hands.

I don't know if you'll give weight to my words, and I understand if you won't, but I share this with hope for us all. I share this knowing I am deeply flawed, that we all are, but we are also the answer.

By the time this reaches you, I hope to have shifted the power over Perean to better hands, and I will be ready to receive you and yours as renewed, true allies. We have a long, hard battle ahead.

Please pass on my warmest sentiments to Doli and Tse.

Thank you for your friendship.
Emanouella

"Thank you for coming all this way."

Emanouella led the young, cloaked woman past a row of bushes and through a hidden door she'd discovered weeks ago in her very own gardens. The torches inside lit the staircase that twisted deep into the earth.

Oskar likely never intended for Emanouella to use these passages to commit treason, but it was the only way to avoid Apollon and his minions.

"I wish I could receive you under better circumstances," she told her visitor. They reached the chamber below, and the woman turned in place. The walls hugged close, and the ceiling sat low. There was hardly room for the two stools she'd set up. "Once your family name and lands have been restored, I promise to make up for it."

The Otuvian princess—an unofficial title for now—pulled her hood forward as if to hide her features, but Emanouella had already glimpsed the beautiful woman beneath. "My father has many reservations he wants me to address on his behalf."

Emanouella smiled. "Then we should begin."

A sharp slap startled half of Court, including Emanouella.

Inside an alcove, just past a wide marble column, Alexandra raised her hand to strike her handmaid a second time.

Emanouella started toward her vicious, cruel daughter, but a large, calloused hand snapped around her wrist.

"Her Majesty the Queen wouldn't want to interfere with matters that are none of her concern."

She met the cold, gray eyes of Apollon Rodelis. "Unhand me."

The temple priest smiled, and his attention lowered to what she held. He snatched her precious envelope from her hand and held it out of her automatic reach.

Fury raged through her. "You have no right—"

"Let's not draw attention," Apollon warned conspiratorially, opening the wordless parchment in full view of everyone in Court. The lone petal fell for the second time. The High Priest bent to retrieve it with his thick, wiry brows drawn together. "What have we here?"

Emanouella hated him, but no more than this very moment. Oskar hadn't reached out in weeks, and her relief at this moment was beyond compare. She had so much to tell him. So much to beg his forgiveness for.

She tore the petal and envelope from Apollon's grasp, crinkling both in her fist. The action immediately drew the hungry gazes of courtiers. "Nothing has changed, Apollon. My business continues to be none of yours."

"Your safety will always be my business."

She wanted to bite that false look of concern off his face. "You should know better than to employ such an act with me. I know who you truly are, or have you forgotten?"

Apollon lengthened and fisted the folds of his robes. He cast a glance around and flashed his teeth. "I shouldn't have to remind you of the recent atrocities that have befallen your own family. Or how we are still without answers. You could be next."

He may as well have stabbed her in the heart. Hot tears sprung to the backs of her eyes. "Don't you dare speak to me of my son." The words sounded as if dragged across gravel. "Get out of my way."

If he said one more word to her, she'd kill him.

He must have read that in her eyes because he wisely bowed his head and stepped aside. But not without a final word. "His Majesty has inquired as to your preparations for Lord Vallou's arrival tomorrow."

"We both know he doesn't care about my cousin's arrival. What is it you're really asking?"

Apollon's lips twitched. "It seems you've been spending much of your time elsewhere lately instead of focusing on your usual duties. Disappearing in the night and early morning. Rarely focused on—"

"Kind of you to be worried for me," Emanouella said for their small audience. She stepped closer and pretended to kiss his cheek. "You should be."

E manouella had come, and she was beautiful, and Oskar's entire purpose for calling her to him vanished. There'd always been something about seeing his queen windblown and out of breath from her travels up the cliff. Arriving in a state she allowed only him to see. Free of poise and care. Flush with color.

Her expression was like watching a flower that had been on the verge of wilting, turning her petals toward the rising sun and the splashes of spring rain. She brightened and glowed with renewed color before his very eyes.

"I came as soon as I could get away," she said. Her eyes sparked as she pushed off the door.

Oskar would never recall those seconds between him standing by that table and when she entered his arms. Her lips tasted like sunlight, and she pushed against him as if suddenly freed of the constraints of a frozen earth. He turned heady in her scents: rose, jasmine, lily, freesia... A woman unfurled.

Her cloak hit the floor, followed by a variety of their belts and weapons. She opened her neck for his mouth and desperately sought the taste of his skin in return. They left a trail of fabric on their way to the bed, a place of whispers, dreams, and passion.

Oskar arranged Emanouella beneath him and kissed his way down her naked body. He paused over her belly and the life within her. The seed they'd planted together. Their love would bloom into a real, tangible thing in just a few months. Time had never been more of the essence.

"My love." Emanaouella's fingers threaded through his hair.

Oskar found her gaze across the plains of her flushed, creamy skin. A line of concern marred the space between her brows.

Things would never be simple for them, would they? Every day, something new and more important stood in their way.

"We have to find a way," he said, her belly warm and soft beneath his palm. "For this life we created."

Emanouella sat up and held his face in her palms. Her gaze opened to soak him in like earth for the rain. "Let's not let anything intrude on this moment we have now. Please, Oskar."

Oskar took her mouth with a kiss so deep, so hungry, that they were forced to share what little breath they had between them. He laid her down, and a heartbeat later, he slid inside her and erased the heartache of the last few weeks.

Later, wrapped in each other, she admitted to everything she'd done with tears sliding silently from her eyes. He wanted to be furious, but how did he have the right? Hadn't he also spent the last few weeks plotting ways to free Mihail Vidalatos?

Tomorrow, it would all be over, and then what? He may very well be on the run with Mihail, searching for the prophesied true heir. Or taking a more direct route to putting Mihail on the throne where he belonged.

That was the goal, at least. Oskar's sole focus was getting to his king, who he could only assume was alive and locked away. Selene had been too silent of late, all but confirming who she found. She should never have avoided him so thoroughly.

By the time Emanouella finished, they were sitting up against the headboard, facing each other with their legs tangled in sheets and each other. Her cheeks were stained red from crying, but she'd lost the quiver in her tone a while ago. She might be sorry for plotting to put their child on the throne as a Vidalatos, but there was no remorse for her plans to help the Perean people.

And only rage toward Orestis and her daughter. Wrath he himself shared. If it wasn't for either of them, he and Emanouella wouldn't be locked behind these walls they had no hope of climbing. They wouldn't be walking on separate, parting paths.

Oskar held his temper in, however, and linked their fingers. "I wish you had trusted me to help."

"I had to do this on my own. I had to do this for my son and my grandsons."

He nodded. "Is this it, then?"

She seemed to understand his question because silver lined her eyes, and her lower lip quivered. "You're the one who said we have a lot of life left. Besides,"—she lifted the ring hanging from a delicate chain around her neck—"we'll always have forever."

* * *

Three Months Ago

"Are you ready?"

Emanouella's heart stuttered, and it had nothing to do with the steaming cavern or the distant, popping earthen fire. Or even the broken octagon of Llinunae Stone beside them.

Today, she would give her soul to the one man who deserved it. She would make a promise that not even Orestis could come between.

She set her hand, palm up, in Oskar's. "I'm ready."

Oskar reached for the blade at his waist but slipped his hand into a pouch instead. A smile slanted across his face. He licked his lips and shifted his weight. "I want to give you something first."

He turned her hand and slid a ring onto her finger, where she typically wore her wedding band. The gold twisting around her finger was split like multiple vines, each topped by tiny blue gems.

"They're flowers," she said, suddenly breathless. "Oskar…"

"You'll never go another winter without a bloom again."

She took his face and kissed him, tears tracking down her cheeks. "All I need is forever with you."

He kissed her and stepped back, taking her hand again. With her palm up, he spun his blade free from the holster. The slice across her skin happened before she realized his intention. The searing pain came a moment later, and she bit back her wince. This was what she wanted.

Blood pooled in her palm as he fisted the same knife and yanked.

Oskar gripped her hand with his own, mixing their life's blood. He swept a thumb across her cheek. "Emanouella, I vow to love you for the rest of this life and into the next."

She stepped closer, and little more than a breath passed between them. "I make you the same vow. I will love you for the rest of this life and into the next."

They shifted their combined hands over the stone and let their blood spill as one onto the Llinunae Stone. The gold veins within the marble pulsed as if drinking their offering. A strange tingling wall of air passed over her, and her ears popped.

Emanouella gasped and looked into Oskar's wide eyes. "Do you feel that? It worked." A laugh burst from her tight chest. "It really worked."

Oskar, beaming, kissed her knuckles. "Forever."

"Forever."

Present Day

They would have forever, but all Oskar wanted was now. *This* life. With her and their child. What hope did he have when there were greater, more dangerous games at play? Had they ever stood a chance?

"I need you to promise me something," he said. "Tomorrow, I need you to keep Selene close. Keep her out of the way. Just in case."

"Why?" She straightened. "What's going on?"

Oskar stroked her cheek and the slope of her chin. Her skin was so soft that it made him hunger for the rest of her again. "I have to get the king's full attention, and I just need you both to be careful. All right?"

Her brows drew together, but she nodded. "Can't you tell me?"

"The truth is, I don't know the extent of what I'll find. Only a hunch." He squeezed her hand. "I will tell you when I know, but things are about to change."

"Why does it sound like you're about to rattle the hornet's nest?"

Oskar frowned. Put that way, and considering her proximity, what was the likelihood of her standing in the crossfire? Would she and their child be the sacrifice he made to make right the wrongs that were started forty years ago?

Emanouella touched his chin, forcing his gaze to return. "How can I help?"

"Keep Selene alive and safe."

"With my final breath."

12

Oskar walked Markos as near the palace as he could, his stomach somewhere near his knees. He'd awoken with a sense of foreboding, heightened only by Emanouella's recent activities. They'd all been for the greater good of Perean, but how would they play out if and when Mihail took back his rightful place?

"Nice day to upset an entire regime," Markos joked, blinking at the cloudless azure sky.

Oskar's face tightened. "Last chance to reconsider."

The young man shook his head. He was about the right age for an heir and the closest to looking like a Vidalatos out of all the men who volunteered. They were all tired of the Perean people suffering for the scraps left by the City Guard and the greedy courtiers increasing rents across their bountiful land. Too many died in the mines for minerals that went into the rare ioprese steel without compensation or even consideration for safer conditions.

"You worry too much, old man," Markos said.

The endearment tightened something in Oskar's chest. He used to call Hristos that. What would the old man say to this?

"The law will keep you safe," Oskar said. "The Council has to hear any and all claims. I just need you to keep everyone distracted long enough for me to slip in and out of the palace unnoticed with Mihail."

For the first time, Markos's mask dropped as he nodded. His chest expanded on a breath. "Just find our king and get him out safely."

"I will. I swear it."

Oskar watched Markos's back until he disappeared into the palace kitchens. They wanted him to be seen by as many people as possible so the king could not erase his arrival or claim without trouble.

Oskar would take the secret tunnels but waited until the palace guard thinned to sneak up to the outer walls to the entrance very few knew about. The dark, musk-scented passage took him up and up and up, around and around, until he came to a second-floor door. From here, he'd have to go through the palace interior and hopefully do so without running into any of the Guard.

Inside the palace, he stepped into a bubble of quiet, his heartbeat a drumbeat in his ears as he quietly shut the hidden door. The tapestry fell back into place, and Oskar made note of its design for later escape. Ivory trees on a slope of the Kirrane Mountains framed the large fabric, and in the distant middle stood the palace as it had been centuries ago.

Markos's voice reached him as if like a familiar hand. "How dare you."

"How dare you," the king growled, and Oskar stiffened. He hurried toward the voices as Orestis continued. "You come here making false accusations. I knew my brother, and I knew very well who he stepped out with."

Oskar approached an alcove open to the foyer below and peered down as Markos said, "This conversation has met its end. I demand to be heard by the Council."

"It isn't that simple," Alexandra said.

Markos was surrounded. Mostly by armed soldiers but also by the royals and palace servants. Good. Witnesses.

Oskar searched for Emanouella, relieved she wasn't in the group below. He found her hidden in a second alcove with Selene and another older woman. As long as they stayed quiet, they should be safe.

Below, Orestis laughed, slow and building like a treacherous tide. Then he aimed at every innocent witness. Without a word spoken, he sentenced them all to death.

Oskar's teeth clenched. It took everything he had to stay silent and still, repeating one word to himself like a prayer: Mihail, Mihail, Mihail.

They knew this could happen. No one could predict Orestis's actions, but this had always been a possibility. The only councilmember there was Apollon, and he would never go against his king.

Down the corridor, Emanouella pulled Selene and the other woman away from the gallery. "Run. Go now before he sees you."

Oskar looked down on Markos again and guilt stabbed him directly in the heart. The Blade had gone pale, and actual disbelief widened his eyes.

"I'm sorry," Oskar whispered, then turned to find his king.

———

Mihail Vidalatos had a son. Markos.

The two souls, with eyes of earth and sky, will set upon a journey to return the lost heir to the land of sea and steel.

Emanouella's mind swam with what that could mean. She must have gone over that line in the prophecy a million times and thought nothing of the implications. None of the lovers had gone on a journey—Selene certainly hadn't.

Was Markos's arrival, his claim, what Oskar had meant by getting the king's full attention? Had *he* found the heir on his own?

She had so many questions and no time to raise any of them. Not until she completed her promise to Selene.

By the time Emanouella arrived in the kitchens, she was out of breath and only a minute—possibly less—ahead of the soldiers Orestis sent to kill the witnesses. "Everyone out." She aimed at the exit to the outside. "Go. Hurry. They're coming."

There were too many, and without the time to fill in any details, only a handful of the servants, cooks, and maids listened. Everyone scattered and ran into each other, into tables, into stools. They knocked over bowls and tripped over sacks of grains.

Ioanna Giannatou, Selene's mother, was one of the furthest from the door and tried to do as instructed. She'd lived here long enough to understand that orders shouldn't be questioned. That damn limp of hers only got her partially through the room by the time the sounds of marching steps reached them.

Emanouella flew to her side and took her hand. "Say nothing."

The woman's eyes had glassed over with unshed tears, but she nodded.

Emanouella's heart was beating too fast, but she faced the opening to the stairs where at least a dozen soldiers appeared.

The guards shoved their swords into the first few people without a word of warning. Following their king's orders without question. Screams bounced off the walls and ripped directly into her chest.

"Stop!" she shouted. "I am your queen and demand you halt this madness."

Her voice shook, but the men did as commanded. One in particular bowed and said, "Your Majesty, we are under King's orders. These people witnessed—"

"They witnessed nothing. Many of us just arrived, and if you'd bothered to ask, you'd know that." She wore her fury like a crown. "Leave this room at once. We have a feast to prepare."

"My Queen—"

"At. Once. How dare you interfere with my business? If the *king* wishes to question me, he may. Until then, you've done quite enough."

The man scanned the room. Girls huddled in groups, shaking and crying. A few boys had ducked behind tables and barrels. Some of the elderly staff stood by and waited for sentencing with their chins lowered. They understood the delicate balance of power here.

Emanouella slammed a fist onto the tabletop. "I said leave!"

The soldier immediately motioned for his men to turn and return up the stairs. He bowed to her. "My Queen."

The air deflated from the room with their retreating steps, and the sobs began anew.

Ioanna sank into her.

"It's all right now," Emanouella said to Ioanna. To the rest. "There shouldn't be any further trouble. Clean up as best you can, and say absolutely nothing of the man who came through here today. Not to yourselves. Not to anyone. Do you understand? *You were not here.*"

She was going to have words with Oskar over this. He risked too many innocent lives today. For what? Nothing was worth all this.

"My daughter?" Ioanna asked.

"She's fine. I sent her to my apartments."

"Thank you."

Emanouella squeezed her hand. "Don't thank me just yet."

Not even she could predict what would happen next.

Oskar couldn't think clearly. Not after everything he'd just learned.

Not after he'd walked away from Mihail, who had been in a physical state Oskar could never have planned for. It would have been impossible to get the rightful king to safety.

And Selene...she was furious with him. Rightly so. He'd messed up. Really messed up. Markos was dead, Mihail would be soon, and all those innocents—

"The danger for us has passed," Emanouella said to Selene in the outer corridor. "The…imposter has been dealt with."

At least Emanouella was safe. He'd nearly collapsed from relief when he heard her voice a moment ago. She'd kept her promise to keep Selene safe too.

All for nothing.

Oskar waited until the way was clear to exit the room.

Emanouella led Selene toward the Royal Wing. "My cousin, Lord Kostas, has arrived. We must see to the final preparations for this evening. Please go speak with Cook. Ensure this incident hasn't affected dinner."

Selene's previous fury vanished like smoke, and she beamed. "She's alive?"

"Go see for yourself."

Oskar ducked into a nearby stairwell and took one step but couldn't go any further. He had to see her. What was one more mistake today?

Emanouella's voice drifted to him a moment later. "I hope it was worth it."

Her cold tone hit him like a lash, opening his skin.

He stepped into the open and bit back the words he wished to say. *I'm sorry. I love you. Forgive me. I made a mistake.* Instead, he went directly to the truth he could finally share. "Mihail Vidalatos is alive. Not for much longer, but he was why I did this. I'm sorry, Em. You have no idea how much."

Her blinks came rapidly. "So it's true, then? Markos was his son?"

"No. He was a decoy. But a child does exist, and they have a legitimate claim to the throne."

She paled, and her hands went to her stomach.

Oskar erased the distance and took her hands, startled by how cold her fingers were. "I know this isn't what you planned, and that's okay. We have a real chance now. We can walk away and raise our child together. Don't you want that?"

Fat teardrops fell from her eyes, and she nodded, though she couldn't—or wouldn't—look at him. "Everything I've done…"

"I know. I'm sorry."

Her tawny eyes flashed. "None of this changes things for Orestis or Alexandra. They will pay for everything they've done."

Oskar didn't know what to say. He would help her if it came to that, but it didn't look like she wanted or needed help. This was something she needed to do on her own.

Still, he reached for her—

Marching steps came up from the stairwell, and Oskar spun, pulling his sword out. He stepped in front of Emanouella just as Orestis, Apollon, and an entire regiment of King's Guard appeared.

The king raised a hand, and the slice of swords rang through the air for the second time today. In the same breath, Oskar saw their deaths as he had the others. The carelessness the king had for innocent lives. He'd kill Emanouella and the child, and Oskar would have to go with them. He couldn't live in a world where she didn't exist.

The king looked Oskar up and down, recognition staying his hand. "Back for more? Didn't you learn your lesson the last time?"

This time, old memories of Hristos lying in his own blood flashed, and the world in Oskar's peripheral clouded.

Oskar aimed the point of his blade at Orestis's throat. "I still owe you for that."

Emanouella's familiar grip took his other hand from behind. "Let him go, Orestis."

Apollon came forward, chuckling to himself, appraising Oskar. "I wondered if that was you sending her those empty messages with nothing but a flower." The priest's gaze shifted to Emanouella. "Is that where you disappeared to last night?"

The king's eyes flared. "What?"

"They've rekindled their little romance," Apollon said.

Orestis pulled his sword free, teeth gritted. "I will kill you myself, Blade."

And Oskar would gladly accept this fight.

Emanouella rushed to stand between the two men, paying the tip of Orestis's blade no mind. Oskar yanked her arm, his heart leaping toward his throat, but she stood her ground with her chin raised.

"You're going to let him walk out of here," she told her husband.

Orestis smirked. "I don't think so."

"You will," she said coldly. "And you'll wait twenty-four hours to even attempt going after him."

"You must think you have something good to buy such a request." His gaze dipped to her belly. "Your bastard child doesn't count. I could have your head for this."

Rage flashed through Oskar, and a warning leapt to his tongue—

"By this time tomorrow," Emanouella said, unphased, "after I've received confirmation that Oskar still lives, I will give you the name you seek."

The king narrowed his eyes. "What name?"

Oskar went ice-cold. There was only one name worth such a hefty price. "Emanouella, no."

She ignored his warning. "The male with eyes of earth and sky. I know his name and who his parents are. I know how you can find him."

Oskar's stomach dropped out.

"You're lying," the king said.

"I was late reaching Selene because I was with *him* first. I helped keep his birth quiet and watched them escape." Emanouella brushed his blade aside as easily as she would grass and closed the distance to her husband. "I can also tell you, you're not ready for the battle you'll have to fight just to breathe his same air."

Orestis Vidalatos lowered his sword and took a single step back. His jaw muscles flared like lightning branches, and his cheeks mottled red. "Let him go."

"Your Majesty," Apollon began, turning towards the king, "we have ways of—"

Oskar put the sword to the priest's throat, halting his words. He'd just seen their "ways," and he would die first. "You won't touch her. Not if you want to keep your secrets from Titos Demakis. My men know what to do."

Orestis's nostrils flared. "I said, let him go."

The King's Guard sheathed their weapons and cleared a path.

But Oskar couldn't go. He couldn't leave Emanouella with these men. The moment he left, how well would his threat keep her safe? Would Orestis care? He'd proven he would do anything to get what he wanted, and nothing would keep him from entering the Ethereal Mountain if and when he was ready.

He *had* to get Selene away from here, and he prayed to the gods her mate never showed his face.

Emanouella turned and dragged Oskar out of earshot. "You can't fight your way out of here. I'll be fine."

Oskar clasped her head and set his lips to her ear, hiding his mouth in her wisps of loose hair. "I'm coming back for you. We'll have that life."

"I know," she whispered, her words sounding choked. "Go. Please."

He met her eyes. "Selene? She won't be safe for much longer."

"Neither of us has ever broken a promise to the other." Her smile wobbled. "I don't intend to start now."

With her life, she'd sworn.

That was what he was afraid of.

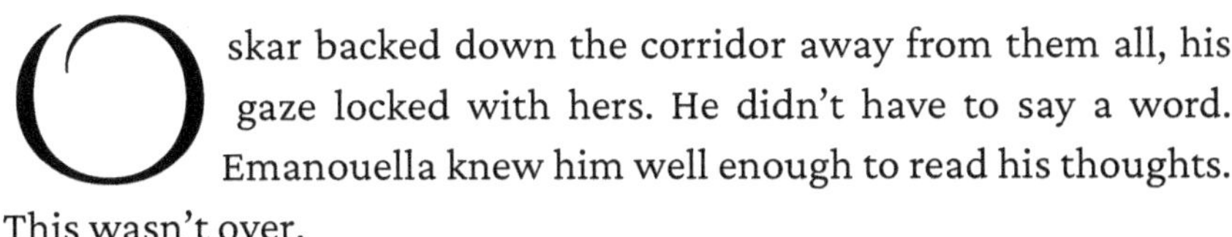

Oskar backed down the corridor away from them all, his gaze locked with hers. He didn't have to say a word. Emanouella knew him well enough to read his thoughts. This wasn't over.

Then he was gone, and she was left cold with the two men she hated most in this world.

"Leave us," Orestis told everyone.

Emanouella braced for the rage coming her way. He would try to force the name out of her; she was sure of it. What he didn't understand was the depth of her love for Oskar. She would rather die than go back on her word. Oskar would be safe for the next twenty-four hours, and Orestis would *never* get that name from her. He would be dead first.

Apollon lowered his chin to the king and said, "Should I stay?"

"No. I would speak with my wife alone."

Orestis held her gaze until each and every echo of footstep vanished. "The child is his?"

"Yes." There was no use denying any of it now. Soon, it wouldn't matter.

"Why bother pretending it was mi—" The truth must have hit him, because his eyes widened. He scrubbed his jaw, laughing silently. "You plan to put that child on the throne."

"I plan to do a lot more than that."

13

Emanouella's feast was a nightmare she couldn't escape. Her hard work in the planning was evident. The dining hall had an ethereal glow throughout. The candlelight sparked off the silver and white. She'd wanted everyone to feel as if they'd stepped through the gates into a god's courtyard, and the ivy winding around the columns did just that. She'd handpicked flowers representing new love and friendship. The fine crystal was as delicate as a cloud, and the silver was lavishly weighted.

The sweet honey wine bubbled, and the fare rose and fell across the tables like a gentle wave. Everything was light yet filling, cool and refreshing, and the courtiers would leave tonight buoyant and dizzy.

She'd wanted this impression for her cousin, and Kostas had dismissed it all as if it were commonplace. Her family, too, had looked past the details as easily as they dismissed her on a daily basis.

That was fine. She was years past needing their validation, and she had larger things to occupy her mind. Like what her next move should be. She'd made friendships and promises to several leaders behind Orestis's back. Had shared secrets about Orestis and Alexandra that came with a deadline. It was all a mess now after Oskar's plan all but erupted the palace into chaos today.

She'd thought Apollon and Orestis had watched her every move before... If she didn't produce the male's name by tomorrow, there was no telling what they'd do to her.

A child does exist, and they have a legitimate claim to the throne.

At least now she understood Orestis's desperation. Why he'd needed the lovers dead. They were meant to find this heir. Did Oskar know where to find them? She wished she'd had time to ask more questions. Like how Mihail Vidalatos was still alive, and did that mean her brother Tiberius lived too? When had Mihail married and conceived an heir, but also, why had he kept it secret?

"I'm curious." Orestis spoke beneath his breath so as not to alert anyone that he dared break his punishing silence toward her. "Why him? What about him made him more worthy of your attention than your own husband? I gave you everything. I protected you, even after catching you with him the first time. I saved his life...*for you.*"

"He isn't afraid to show me how he feels, and that's the difference. You spend so much time warding yourself against hurt and loss that you'll never truly be happy." Anger rose within her like water slowly releasing from a cracking dam. "And please don't pretend you did any of that for me when you've spent decades protecting your claim to the throne. A seat at the head of a table, husband. The power to make decisions over an entire nation—poorly, I might add, as half of them are starving. Do you have any idea how small that makes you?"

"As small as you, I imagine, after you got yourself with another man's child and plotted to overthrow me. How do you intend to do that with our daughter next in line? Will you have your lover kill her? You're no better than me."

She gave him a secret smile and leaned closer. "You're not truly worried, are you? What of Mihail's child?"

A laugh leapt up his throat. "That man is dead and no longer a concern. Neither is Mihail."

So Mihail was dead now, too. She hadn't known him, but her stomach sank anyway. What Orestis also revealed was that the truth remained hidden. He hadn't rid himself of Mihail's heir at all. He only *thought* he had. That was a lie she would let him believe.

"And tomorrow," he continued, "you'll give me that one name I need to finally put all of this to bed. Then I can focus on—what was that concern of yours? Filling the bellies of my starving people. No credit at all for the Navy I've built to protect our lands. Your brother benefits heavily from that, by the way."

"My brother uses you, and once your value has run out... What do you think he'll do then?"

His teeth flashed with a feral smile. "Maybe I'll put you and your cousin between myself and his blade. How about that?"

"After all these years, you still believe he cares. I'm almost sorry for you, husband."

Down the table, Kostas's chair hit the ground like a crack of thunder, capturing the entire room's attention. Nothing that occurred after that was a surprise to anyone, least of all Emanouella. Of course, Alexandra acted like a vicious snake, and of course, Orestis would use this opportunity to exert his dominance.

But then Alexandra focused on Selene and said the words that made Emanouella's blood run cold. "I think you'll soon learn that I never forgive, nor do I forget. Isn't that right, Selene?"

Selene paled from her quiet place along the back wall, and she'd never looked more fragile.

Emanouella's promise came roaring through her, barbed and tightly wrapped. All this time, she'd been watching Orestis for potential moves against the girl and hadn't given her daughter a second thought.

That damned dinner. Alexandra had nearly killed Selene, and Orestis had beat her with his own hand... Alexandra hadn't let that slight go. She wouldn't.

They had to leave this dinner. Now.

As Emanouella suspected, Selene knew much more than she'd let on and hadn't seemed at all surprised when Emanouella revealed the danger she was in. If she could get the girl and her mother to Oskar, he would know what to do. Maybe if he knew the boy's name, too, he could connect the lovers and find the heir.

In the meantime, Emanouella had no idea what her next move was other than to do everything in her power to remove Orestis and Alexandra from the gods' gameboard. It was the very least she could do for Oskar and Selene. And Augustus, wherever he was.

Alexandra confirmed her suspicions by appearing outside her apartments. Selene's hold on Emanouella's arm tightened, but Emanouella had been playing this game with her daughter for a while now. She remained calm and careful not to let her tension show.

"Alexandra? Is there something you need?" The blood of an innocent, perhaps?

"No. I was just taking a walk before retiring for the night." She kissed Emanouella's cheeks with cold lips. "Goodnight, Mother."

Emanouella shivered just as Alexandra added a final farewell. "Sweet dreams, Selene."

They watched the princess go in stunned silence.

"Everything will be all right," Emanouella said. "But maybe you should sleep in my rooms tonight."

Selene shook her head. "I couldn't do that, Your Majesty. If anyone were to catch me—"

"If you're worried about Roya, don't be." That woman wouldn't have a position here much longer, either. She was a menace, but she was also Apollon's informant. Ridding the palace of her would take a special sort of care and timing.

Selene guided them into the apartments and closed the door. "Alexandra... Her ways are much more inventive than sneaking into a room and stabbing someone in their sleep. The aftermath is the part she enjoys. The shock, and how she can play into that."

Emanouella stopped. Selene kept her gaze lowered, and her body was half-turned away, shoulders tense. She'd spoken against a royal, and she'd never have done that before. It would have gotten her killed in Alexandra's service. What else had she seen? Survived?

"Selene, I'm so sorry. I wish I'd known. I could have protected you better."

A weak smile shifted her mouth. "Don't apologize. I'm just glad you know the truth. I've wanted to tell you for so long but didn't know how."

"I understand." Emanouella tucked a loose wave of blond behind her ear. "I'll ask the men to watch your rooms tonight. Just in case."

"That would be kind of you. Thank you." Selene gave her a true smile then. "Enough about me. Let's get you and that precious babe into bed."

Later, alone in her apartments, the quiet wrapped over Emanouella like a chilly cloak. The veranda doors were open to the breeze drifting off Castona Bay, and the moon was so close to full that she could see her bluff tonight.

One day soon, she would give all of this up—the subterfuge, the expectations—and live a content life with Oskar in their little cottage. She would lay in the field of wildflowers every day and go to bed each night with the man she loved. Together they would raise a child who smiled because they were happy and laughed because they felt like it and ran into the wind for no reason at all.

The dream warmed her for the first time in hours. Maybe even days. It'd been too long since she felt such a deep sense of *hope*.

Emanouella closed the doors and faced her quiet, taper-lit rooms. The painting of her son was too shadowed for details, but his visage would always be in her mind, forever handsome and kind. He didn't deserve such a cruel ending.

Speaking of her vicious daughter.

Alexandra had been in her rooms and something Selene said... Her daughter enjoyed the aftermath. The shock. Her reaction after the headless bodies arrived hit a whole new way now. The tears had come from too-clear eyes. The wails hadn't been deep enough. And yet, everyone held her and soothed her and made gentle promises to keep her safe.

Emanouella's bedside water jug had been the sixth place she looked, and still, she almost missed it. A glass of clear water had conveniently been poured. Just in case, she imagined.

Emanouella pulled one of the petals out of the water and shook her head. Dyphis Flower. The number of petals inside the jug was overkill, and it sickened her to think of Alexandra's ultimate goal. She would not only kill her child but Emanouella herself. Emanouella had made a mistake that day in using the baby as a weapon to Alexandra's potential rule. She'd all but put a target on them both.

She picked up the water jug and started for the bathing chamber.

Apollon entered her room without so much as a knock. A man who saw no barriers. A man who didn't fear repercussions. "Good evening."

She stumbled to a stop. "Get out of here. How dare you?"

"Sit, Emanouella." He motioned for her bed. "We have much to discuss, you and I."

The lack of honorifics made her heart pound. He no longer felt them necessary. She was certain to find out why momentarily, but fighting him wouldn't do her any good.

She returned the jug, and for a moment, she considered offering him a glass of water.

He quickly squashed that idea. "I wouldn't drink that. I hear Alexandra was here earlier. With the petals of a Dyphis Flower is my understanding."

Just how closely were his people watching now, and when had they begun to include Alexandra's activities?

Alexandra was usually more careful, and Apollon wasn't *so* hard to fool. After all, she'd been doing it for decades. The fact that he was here now only meant one thing.

"Roya and I need to have a long talk," she said and sat on the edge of the bed. She pulled her robes closed over her knees and chest.

"Don't blame her for alerting me to the potential danger to your life." He chuckled silently to himself. "She only wants you safe and well."

"She only wants to remain in your good graces. But, do go on, Apollon. Why are you here? If it's the male's name you're after, you have several hours remaining."

"I already have the name."

A cannonball could have hit her square in the stomach and not felt as bad as the knot twisting her gut.

"It's a long story," he continued with a wave of the hand, then withdrew a folded page of parchment. "Augustus Triarius and his ship, the *Soris*, will dock in the morning. Apparently, he's here on a job and has no idea the net we're preparing to cast for him."

Ice-cold water slunk through her veins. This couldn't be happening.

Apollon opened the doors to her bedside terrace, and the breeze ruffled his hair and robes. "I appreciate all the trouble you went to for the lovers. You've played the game very well. I truly admire your tenacity, which is why I'm telling you this. It's the least I could do."

It was more likely that he wanted to brag about his latest accomplishment. "Then you're a fool. I could leave and warn Oskar the moment you're gone."

He lifted a full, wiry brow. "Your usual exits are already being watched. And we've increased the number of men on patrol. Any efforts you make will be futile." He smirked. "We may not be able to get our hands on your lover now, but we will. Your husband looks forward to the day you watch us take his head. Will you hold it the way you did Angelos's?"

Bile climbed her throat, and she forced herself to swallow. Begged the memories to stay buried. She had to stay focused. "You're dreaming if you think Oskar so easily within reach. Even if it means I never see him again, you will never find him."

"Something tells me he'll be the first to stand between Augustus and our men." His eyes gleamed, and his smile turned arrogant. "Am I wrong?"

The world spun as his words tore everything apart. Every sacrifice, plan, vow...for nothing. Orestis would still get his way.

Oskar *would* protect Augustus, especially once he learned the King's Guard scoured the city and docks for a certain captain with eyes of blue and brown. He'd employ the entire Guild in this battle, and her people would be caught in the crossfire. The odds of Orestis hauling the lovers up to the mountain were still too great.

What could she do? She couldn't just sit here. She'd made vows to Angelos's spirit, to herself, to Oskar—

"Keep Selene alive and safe."

"With my final breath."

Grief hit with the weight of a battering ram, destroying everything. She held her stomach and swallowed the pit of sand in her throat.

"Leave my rooms, Apollon," she said, voice quivering. "You've had your moment. You've won. We're done here."

For once, he didn't argue. "Good night, Emanouella. Sleep well."

The door clicked shut, and a hot tear rolled over her lower lid. The drop tickled her cheek on the way down and dripped off her chin into her lap.

She held her belly, her child, her last love. "Please forgive me."

A sob broke from her chest. Apollon and Orestis would never be finished with her. Not after this. They could execute her for treason on the merits of infidelity alone. She doubted her threats would stop them in the end. She'd interfered too much and had her finger on too many strings.

There was only one thing she could do, and the landslide that followed—

She didn't care about the ultimate fallout that would hit several corners of their world. Only that Oskar received the help he needed, and she could do that in the form of a major disruption. Something so big that the entire palace—all of Perean—would be divided and distracted.

Emanouella's water glass sparkled in the candlelight, and the ring hanging on the chain beneath her robes heated against her skin. Searing tears prickled behind her eyes.

This life had always worked against them, and it wouldn't stop.

If the gods were good and cared at all, the next life wouldn't.

With shaking fingers, she reached for the glass and took great, gulping swallows of the poison, tears leaking from her eyes.

With a shaky breath, she returned the glass and scrubbed the back of her hand across her wet mouth. She didn't feel any different, but it wouldn't be long.

Emanouella stood and strode from her room. She sat at the small table with its neat stack of parchment and quills.

She took one sheet and began to write just as her nose began to bleed.

14

The chaos began with a whisper. Like a breath of air across his skin that raised gooseflesh in warning.

Oskar remained calm through it all, something that was second nature after all these years. Panic wouldn't help him find the male that was in the market somewhere. It wouldn't reverse time to a point where the king learned of his arrival. The whys and hows made no difference, only that it was.

He scattered his Blades throughout the streets, ordering the men to protect the people where they could and keep an eye out for the man with one blue eye and one brown. There was a time when the men would have questioned such a thing, but they knew much of the truth now. They had all seen Selene and her strange eyes. Some, the older ones, had been around long enough to remember Aura and Vasilis. And they all held onto hope that a true heir would arrive.

Oskar quickly found the pirate slinking through the streets with an eye patch and knew he'd found him. He was the right age— twenty—and the patch was a dead giveaway. To him, at least. He stood out for other reasons too. The male was above average in height and appearance and his overall bearing screamed *look at me!*

He would look perfect at Selene's side, though now wasn't the time to consider such things. Oskar had to get the two of them out of the city alive. Then, he would let them work that part out for themselves.

Oskar caught up to the pirate, yanked him by the collar, and spun him into the shadows, where he bounced him against a wall. Oskar assumed the man would fight back, so he braced an arm across his chest. He just needed enough time to say what he—

The pirate discharged a grin that made Oskar tense. The fucking man had put a knife to *his* throat. Unbelievable. There hadn't been a sound or noticeable shift in the lad's movements to indicate it. Absolutely incredible. So much so that he wouldn't put him on his ass.

Yet.

"I haven't met many outside my guild who've pulled a blade that fast. I'm impressed."

"You should see how fast I can slit a throat."

"You don't want to do that."

"The next words out of your mouth need to give me a damn good reason why not."

Oskar grinned. "It's not I the king hunts for, and you're going to need all the help you can get."

He had the man's full attention after that but for some expected hesitation. It wasn't until the mention of Selene that the pirate fully gave over. Oskar was surprised, actually, that she already held sway over him.

And finally, Oskar heard the words Emanouella had long held to herself.

"Captain Augustus Labienus Triarius."

Augustus.

Oskar's throat nearly closed. He gripped Augustus's shoulder rather than succumbing to the need to hug the familiar soul before him. "It's nice to see you again, old friend."

Unsurprisingly, Augustus looked at him as if he were mad. "We've never met."

"I'm happy to tell you everything, but first, we must get you somewhere safe."

A series of alarm bells sounded from the palace, and Oskar's entire body flashed with cold. He barely let himself register if Augustus kept up as he raced over rooftops and down alleyways. Instinct took over as he climbed walls and leapt rooftops.

Oskar could fathom a few reasons for calling back the King's Guard, and none of them were good. Today, however, there was one person just as important as Augustus. Selene. The king couldn't risk losing either of them, and he would fight to hold onto the one in his custody.

Still, he needed confirmation, and his men would likely already have answers.

He came across Panos atop a roof, and the Blade lowered his hood, revealing thick black hair. The look on his face told Oskar everything he needed to know. The news wasn't good.

"Tell me," Oskar said. He refused to believe the king would hurt Selene, but he'd also seen the lengths he'd go to to keep someone alive. "Is Selene all right?"

Panos frowned. "She's missing."

"Missing?"

"Oskar... Selene has been accused of poisoning the queen."

The words landed in a messy pile. Just clunky pieces with no sense. The queen. Accusations. Selene. Poison?

He had to get to Emanouella. He had to see if she was okay—

"Queen Emanouella is dead."

"What?" His mind and body broke apart. It was as if a great quake struck cruelly and with great fury. Part of him was left on one side, forever separated from the other. The entire world shook with aftershocks, and he stumbled back a step. *What?*

The ghost of a hand landed on his shoulder, and somewhere very far away, Panos said, "I'm sorry."

But Oskar could only see Emanouella spinning and laughing in the field of flowers. See her smile parting the clouds. Watch her break free of the chains life had bestowed upon her at birth. He could still smell the wildness of a whole world on her skin.

"Is it Selene?" Augustus practically tripped crossing the roof, hauling Oskar out of his memories. "What's happened?"

The words came, though he wasn't sure how. "The queen is dead. She was poisoned."

Her. His child. *Their* child. They created an entire life from their love, and someone snatched it away without a second thought. His family was gone. Gone. No heartbeat, no breath, no smile or laughter or holding of hands.

"Selene Marinea stands accused of the queen's murder," Panos said on that distant plane of existence Oskar couldn't reach. "The princess has ordered her execution."

Orestis did this. And Apollon, who couldn't leave it alone. He saw the power he could wield in a prophecy and used that to his advantage. The two of them played with their lives for decades, and Emanouella got swept up in their game.

Oskar clenched his fists and made one final vow to the gods, to the world, to Emanouella.

They wouldn't get away with this.

***

The sun set on the blood spilled all over the palace grounds.

The battle was over, at least, and the lovers were safe. Selene was in the best hands possible with Augustus. Oskar still couldn't believe the web the Fates wove with this pair. Cassia Rutiliana was his mother. Of all the families to be born from... He'd never forget the day she and her twin accepted their destiny.

Oskar ventured through the palace like a man without his soul. The familiar pathways, walked only the day before, had him slipping toward grief every few minutes, but he fought it like he would any other battle. He would stay focused if for no other reason than to keep himself alive long enough to put the king and his priest in the fucking ground.

He wasn't fool enough to believe that a possibility would be here and now. He was a patient man—his time would come eventually. When it happened, he would at least be able to look each man in the eye. They would know who Oskar honored with their demise.

After he did this one thing for Selene. She'd been through too much for her mother. Had lost and given, and he'd made excuse after excuse. It seemed selfish now, especially after learning that he was too late.

The king had Ioanna taken to the executioner's courtyard for "questioning." He planned to burn answers out of her, not knowing or caring that Ioanna didn't know anything.

Oskar watched long enough to nock the arrow as she burned and prayed Selene would forgive him.

***

The old healer, Athena, unlocked the thick wooden door and frowned. "I cleaned her as best I could." She squeezed Oskar's hand with gnarled knuckles, and his knees nearly gave out.

Not yet. Not here.

"Thank you," he said to his old friend. Her father had been a Blade long, long ago and she was easily his most trusted palace informant.

"You have time," Athena said as he walked through the door. "I'll be out here should trouble come your way."

The door shut, and Oskar faced the quiet corridor.

The lower levels of the palace were cool and sparsely lit. Last he was here, he hung from the ceiling and watched Hristos die. He'd walked away, barely, and didn't touch Emanouella again for over twenty years.

No one was here now.

No one living.

Oskar's stomach turned with every step, and dread crawled across his skin every time he looked into one of the many rooms. Soldiers were spread across tables, frozen and gray. Few without arms or legs or heads. The battle had been vicious, and the Guild's dead were in similar condition.

These men weren't why he was here.

He found her at the very end.

Someone had surrounded her with soft, flickering candlelight. She was clean and had been redressed. A glittering, delicate crown, not unlike the one he first saw on her, sat atop her head. Her skin had been dusted with gold to match her chiton.

From the doorway, she could have been sleeping.

He stumbled over to wake her—

This wasn't sleep. He knew her in sleep as well as he knew her in the light of day.

Oskar choked and retched, and he couldn't feel his legs. He gripped the cold slab as the floor tilted.

She didn't smell right. Like a damp flower that had rotted under too much sun.

Whoever cleaned her hadn't gotten all the dried blood from her nose. No amount of makeup could cover the burst vessels beneath her cheeks and under her eyes.

And her skin...

Oskar took her stiff, cold hand and she didn't take his back. Her eyes didn't open. There was no warm sigh to greet him. She wasn't here.

Why wasn't she here?

A sob ripped free from his tight chest and took the remains of his soul with it. His entire world lay across this table, a sucking vortex stripping him of hope and bliss and an entire future. His family.

Someone looked at this unimaginably selfless creature and erased her. For what? A crown and a title?

Emanouella's other hand blurred where it lay over her stomach, and Oskar caressed the gentle swell beneath. That was the moment the vortex hungrily took his dreams, too. Those imaginings he'd allowed himself. A tiny little fist squeezing his finger and, later, the small hand reaching for guidance. A life with her eyes and depth of love, and maybe his gentle patience.

Oskar squeezed her hand until her ring cut into his palm. The sound of paper crinkled—

He froze and blinked the blur from his eyes.

She wore his ring. He'd paid handsomely for the special request, wanting a band that looked like the flowers she loved so much.

Her wearing it now—at all—didn't make sense. She never wore it in the palace. She wouldn't have dared.

He flipped Emanouella's hand, and there, tucked into the band, was a small bit of parchment.

Oskar tugged the ring off her finger and unrolled the slip.

"I kept my promise," it said.

A fresh lump clogged his throat, and he stepped closer to the head of the table. He smoothed her hair, letting the tears fall. "Yes, you did, my love."

EPILOGUE

Shadi Silver Wolf, Matriarch of Yiria, lowered the missive that had been penned weeks ago. The second sheet of parchment —a quickly penned report—dashed the momentary swell of hope. She and her people had been left alone for so long—left to struggle, to fight their own battles. And this woman, whom she'd met more than twenty years ago, had held out her hand.

Due to the agonizingly slow communication between Yiria and the rest of the world, the news arrived too late.

"What is it?" Doli, unable to contain her curiosity, handed off one of their granddaughters to free her arms. She hurried across the room and gently touched Shadi's arm. "Who has written? What does it say?"

"Emanouella Vidalatos is dead."

Doli froze. "How awful."

"She wrote just before to offer her allegiance. She speaks of why King Vidalatos and their daughter Alexandra cannot be trusted."

Doli lifted Emanouella's letter and read in silence. "These are powerful accusations. Do you believe her?"

Like Emanouella, Shadi recalled the other woman fondly, if not sadly. She had sensed strength within the young queen that the king did his best to squash. Shadi had wanted to spend time with Emanouella, maybe offer her friendship and courage. Things hadn't worked out to their advantage, however, and they never saw each other again.

"I believe her," Shadi said. "I must speak with the Eternal One. In the meantime, gather the council. We must prepare."

"For what? They are on the other side of the world."

"That doesn't make us invisible. As long as we have something of value to offer, this king is not to be trusted, most especially if he is indeed in league with the gods." Shadi folded the parchment in half, then again. "It's time we learned who our true allies are, and how we can return our hand of friendship to this queen."

<hr>

Chrysanthi disembarked from the skiff, her unsteady steps guided by a mysterious sailor. After enduring months at sea, the stability of dry land was a disorienting shift, causing her stomach to churn.

The man's smile quirked. "Sea legs. It'll pass."

She swallowed the thick ball of acid and attempted a smile in return. "Can you tell me how to get to the palace?"

His thick brows drew together, and she understood his confusion. She wasn't a royal and nowhere near a courtier. She wasn't even moderately wealthy, though Emanouella Vidalatos had given her enough coin to live the rest of her life without worry.

"The palace?" the man echoed, his voice tinged with surprise. "What business could you possibly have there?"

Chrysanthi touched the pouch on her hip. Inside was the final promise she'd made Emanouella upon her departure over twenty years ago. A letter to be delivered in the event of Emanouella's untimely death.

"I have something for King Demakis from the late queen of Perean."

O skar held his breath and silently prayed as Selene focused on the distant target. She held the knives in a loose but controlled grip, flipped one blade, pinched the tip, and threw. She didn't wait for it to land, putting everything into her full body spin, flipped the next knife, pinched, and threw.

Both blades hit the target.

Up and down the training field, Guild Blades and acolytes erupted in applause.

Warmth and pride filled Oskar's chest. He'd always known Selene had it in her to get this. Was it a perfect shot? No. But they didn't fly past. Nor did they bounce off. Lately, the first struck fine. It was the second throw that went way off course.

A Guild brother approached her with a smile, gave her a firm pat on the shoulder, and then instructed her further. It was time to focus on her aim.

The Guild had prioritized her training in the few weeks since Selene agreed to stay and help Dimitrios. Whether they were grateful for her part in returning Mihail's lost heir or had simply warmed to her, Oskar had never witnessed a greater group effort. His men treated her like a cherished sister.

For Oskar, Selene was his family. She may not be his blood, but he loved her. He found the idea of her leaving—no matter how distant in the future—was already burrowing a deep hole in his chest.

Hours later, Oskar walked Selene back to the palace through the marketplace. Past corners and doorways with the ghosts of his and Emanouella's past. She was absolutely everywhere.

Months ago, he'd contemplated following Emanouella into their next life. To this day, he ached for the right time to reveal itself. He was ready, if not for Selene and Augustus.

They didn't need his protection anymore; that much was clear. But he wouldn't leave Selene defenseless. Emanouella gave her life to keep her safe, and so would he. He would see her training through until the day she stepped on the Entia and sailed into the unknown world. And then, only then, would he go.

Selene paused outside a cart of flowers to buy a bouquet, and the seller thanked her by name. Several others waved to her from afar. She graced each and every one of them with her kind smile, waving as they left.

"The people love you," Oskar noted when they were out of earshot.

Selene smirked, and the expression was similar to one he'd noted on Augustus many times. On the male, he tolerated it. On Selene, he found it charming. "The people love that I have coins in my pocket."

Maybe for some. But she didn't spend as much as she thought she did. It had everything to do with the time she spent in the market. She conversed with complete strangers and walked away knowing their names. She danced and laughed and crowned children with flower rings she made on request. Like Emanouella before her, she arrived at the temple to help hand out food and clothing to the poor.

Witnessing her live without fear and become who she was meant to be would have made her mother proud.

"How are things with Augustus?" he asked.

A blush filled her cheeks. "They're...good."

Oskar laughed. "I know that look. I've *felt* that look. You're insanely happy."

"Yes, but hold on. You've 'felt that look'? Oskar Dahlin, have you been in love before?"

The warmth seeped right out of him as if a plug had been pulled, and his throat tightened.

Selene, ever observant, took hold of his hand and stopped him. "I'm sorry. You don't have to tell me if you don't want to."

The weight of twenty-two years landed on his shoulders, and he sank onto the nearest crate.

"Oskar?"

"I'm all right." He scrubbed his jaw, coarse with beard shadow, and shook his head. "No, that's a lie. I'm far from all right."

Selene perched on a barrel of honey-sweetened wine and took his hand. If he closed his eyes, he could imagine that was Emanouella sitting there offering to share his grief. Trust like that didn't come often, but Oskar knew that Selene would hold his admission in confidence in the same way Emaounella once had.

"The child Emanouella carried? It was mine."

Selene's eyes flew wide, and she covered her gasp with her hand.

"The affair began before you were born, and circumstances forced us apart that I will regret for the rest of my days. It wasn't until Angelos died that we rekindled our friendship, and that quickly became more."

Tears lined Selene's eyes, sparking his own. Blinking, he focused on his hands clasped before him and summarized their brief relationship as best he could. By the end, he revealed Emanouella's ring, which he wore on a chain beneath his tunic.

Selene didn't utter a word until he finished. "Now I understand why you went after Apollon so furiously in the mountain. I've wanted to ask but didn't think it was my business."

Oskar sucked in a deep inhale, heat kindled anew. He would never stop being angry at Apollon and Orestis for what they did. "I couldn't let him draw another breath. Not after everything."

Selene bit her lip. A line furrowed between her brow, and Oskar sensed she was holding back questions.

"It's all right to be curious," he said. "After all we've been through, Selene, I count you among my closest friends. If there's something you wish to ask, go ahead."

"Are you sure?" On his nod, she went on. "It's just that... What about Alexandra?"

"What about her?"

"You had an opportunity to face her in the mountain. If you did that because you felt I deserved retribution more—"

"What are you talking about?" An icy cold weight formed in his chest.

"The Dyphis Flower."

The method with which Emanouella had been poisoned. He'd never questioned it, and now...? Why hadn't he questioned it? Why was Selene talking about *Alexandra*?

Selene's hands quivered, and teardrops tumbled over her eyelids. "I thought you knew."

"Selene. I need you to say the words." Oskar struggled to keep his body still when he really wanted to sprint all the way to Soterra, find Alexandra, and strip her slowly of all her skin. "I have to hear you say it."

"Oskar, I'm so sorry." She grasped his hand. "It was the princess. Alexandra poisoned Emanouella."

The air burst from his lungs, followed by a hollow laugh, and suddenly he had one more thing to live for.

Vengeance.

...to be continued in
A Clash of Steel

DEAR READER

Thank you for being here!

As I was writing this, Oskar and Emanouella's story felt much, much larger, but due to timing constraints of my own making, I had to keep it short!

Maybe one day I'll dive back in and give them the page time they deserve, but for now, I hope this fills in a lot of the blanks and sets the tone for what's coming next!

If you're inclined to review this book, please know your thoughts— good or bad—are safe. I only ask that you don't tag me in the nega- tive ones.

Thank you so much!!

Misty

A Clash of Steel
Book 2 of A Sea of Echoes

The spark of war.

The separation of Lovers by oceans and seas isolates a vulnerable king. Those are the words haunting Augustus Triarius at night. Three months at Court with Selene have proven that she was worth leaving the pirate fleet for, even if his life as the would-be king's loyal companion holds no true purpose. But fate intervenes once again, and Selene disappears at the hands of an old enemy. A desperate fight to see her returned forces Augustus back into the world of piracy, and immersed in a war that will determine the fate of the Triarius fleet.

A king without a crown.

Dimitrios Vidalatos never planned to seek the Perean throne, let alone have his fate as king held hostage. Until the inquisitor officially declares him king, half of the country stands behind his cousin, Alexandra Vidalatos, as does the might of the Soterran army. Isolated in a foreign land, thwarting assassination attempts at every turn, and the Lovers lost to the seas, Dimitrios must seek new allies. And as a king without a crown, he has little to offer, and no hope of keeping his people safe.

A past that won't be forgotten.

Selene Marinea won't be anyone's bait, least of all pirate captain Tristan Thorne's. After a daring escape leads her to follow the tug of her Lover's bond, she expects to find Augustus at the other end. Instead she faces Roman Cardoso, a man who claims there's more to the story of the Lovers than what she's been told. And with him, an entire civilization of blue-and-brown-eyed people just like her. They open their arms to her with an offer to return her soul into their fold. On one condition: she must leave Augustus behind.

As battles are waged for thrones on land and sea, Selene's trial is for her soul and the heart that Roman says never truly belonged to Augustus. She was *Roman's* soulmate all along.

IN THIS SERIES

The Series

A Sea of Echoes
A Clash of Steel
The Way of Souls
The Will of Gods

From the world of
A Sea of Echoes

A Casualty of Wildflowers
...and more to come

Also by Misty D. Waters

Charming Dove Harbor

Checking Yes

Tell Me No Lies

Absolutely Maybe

OTHER WORKS BY M.D. WATERS

Archetype

Prototype

PRAISE FOR M.D. WATERS

M.D. Waters has given us that rare and wonderful action heroine who possesses both nerve and emotional depth. That rich characterization combined with an intricately crafted sci-fi mystery made *Arch*etype an enthralling debut that I couldn't put down.

— #1 *NEW YORK TIMES* BESTSELLING AUTHOR
RICHELLE MEAD

A twisty, thought-provoking futuristic tale that unnerves and enthralls.

— FAMILY CIRCLE

Readers looking for a great thriller with a strong female protagonist mixed with a hint of science fiction should pick this up immediately.

— LIBRARY JOURNAL (STARRED REVIEW)

Archetype is the literary equivalent of a big-screen block-buster with its beautiful but deadly heroine, tragic love triangle and grim futuristic setting. The closest thing in print may by Margaret Atwood's *The Handmaid's Tale*, but Emma is Offred with mixed martial arts training...*Archetype* finished with a cliffhanger made even more tantalizing by Dutton's promise to publish the sequel, *Prototype*, in six months. The prospect has me more excited than the next "Hunger Games" movie.

— *ASSOCIATED PRESS*

A chilling, action-packed futuristic thriller....Like the works of Margaret Atwood, *Archetype* has kept me thinking about it and the questions it raises long after having turned the last page.

— BILLIE BLOEBAUM, POWELL'S BOOKS

A mystifying tale that tiptoes up and grabs you by the throat....With writing that is supremely confident, Waters builds the tension slowly and Emma's doubts and secrets multiply until the haunting explosion of the truth.

— SUSAN WASSON, BOOKWORKS